Dancing

Suspended in Air

Johanna Schwartz

Dancing, Suspended in Air is a work of fiction. Any association with real people or places is purely coincidental or is used in a fictitious manner. The story is set in the late 1950s early 1960s. Some words and/or phrases, such as "Negro" are, therefore, representative of that time period.

Published by Piscataqua Press
32 Daniel St., Portsmouth, NH 03801
www.ppressbooks.com

ISBN: 9781950381364

Printed in the United States of America

Hello, Dear Reader,

I am so glad you have chosen to read my book. You don't have to read or understand the names of the jazz steps or the French terms for the ballet steps, positions etc. to enjoy *Dancing, Suspended in Air*. Please just skip over them. There is, however, a glossary of ballet/jazz terms at the end of the book if you wish to know what they mean. All the words in the glossary are underlined in the text.

Part One

Best Friends, 1959

"Oh, *wow*, I can't believe tomorrow we'll *finally* know Mrs. Evans's surprise! It's all I've thought about for the past week," I said to Laura, who stood at her bureau fishing through her jewelry box for her favorite earrings.

"I wonder what it is 'cause it's got to be *extra special*."

"That's for sure! Maybe she's taking us to the movie *The Red Shoes*, or Mrs. Evans is having classes during the week. She might have a ballerina give us a class." My mind swirled with a million possibilities. Before I knew it, I was leaping and twirling around Laura's bedroom.

Seeing me, she said, "Hey, I've got an idea. Let's use my mom's makeup kit; she won't mind. We'll look like we're ballerinas! I'll put on your makeup."

"Oh, no, you can't. My mother will *absolutely kill me* if I wear makeup. She says I'm not old enough."

"Ah, *come on!*" insisted Laura, heading toward her parents' bedroom. "You're almost thirteen for heaven's sake. Just wipe the makeup off before you leave. Your mom won't know. Sit down," she directed, pulling the chair away from her mother's dressing table. I sat down but abruptly turned away from the mirror to avoid seeing my drooping left eyelid. It was closed at birth and opens only partway now. Recently, it had been embarrassing me. Laura, unaware of my wariness, quickly rubbed a greasy foundation base over my face, and then patted a sweet-smelling powder around my cheeks. Little particles of soft silky powder cascaded down my neck. It felt pleasant, but I grew very uneasy when Laura began applying the eye makeup.

To keep my discomfort away, I said, "Know what? A few weeks ago, Mrs. Evans told mom that I have a dancer's body and, if I really work hard, I could become a ballerina. I'm seriously thinking about it. Have you thought about a ballet career? I mean *really* thought about it, not like some little kid who is fantasizing?"

"You know I have! Haven't we always wanted to be ballerinas?"

"Sure, we have. I just mean that it's different now. Being a ballerina isn't pretend for me anymore."

"It's not pretend for me either. Think of it, we could become real ballerinas dancing in the same ballet company, traveling the world together, performing before thousands of people."

"Yah, we'd see each other every day for classes and rehearsals. If we were touring, we could share a hotel room."

"Sounds great. There, I'm done. Open your eyes."

I held my breath, and then took a cautious look. "Wow, what did you do? I look terrific," I lied. Honestly, I wanted to cry. The eye shadow accented my drooping eyelid, making my face look crooked. If only I looked like everyone else.

"Oh, Jo, you *do* look fabulous," said Laura. She bent down and gave me a quick hug.

"Thanks, Laura. You're my very best friend."

We had been best friends since she moved here in second grade. I had never told Laura why my eyelid droops and she never asked. For years we played outside, swinging on my swing set or playing croquet. Now a bit older, we listened to records or watched "American Bandstand" on television. I preferred to play outside, but I would *never* tell Laura. She'd think I was acting childish.

We attended Oyster River Junior High School in Durham, where the University of New Hampshire was located. It was a small town with only a few stores. I lived a half-mile walk from school, but Laura took the bus. In elementary school, we were always in the same classroom but, now that we were in seventh grade, she was in seven A – that's the smart kids' class – and I was in seven B – the average kids' class. So, we met outside our homerooms, before the first bell rang, to chat. We connected at recess, lunch, and after school whenever we could.

"Will Liz let me try on her old <u>tutu</u>, the one she wore for that recital?" I inquired.

Liz, Laura's older sister, gave up ballet two years ago. She was fifteen and dating boys.

"Let's ask her. I doubt she'd care."

Laura pushed Liz's bedroom door open. The pungent odor of nail polish flooded the room. Liz sat on her bed painting her toes, a *Seventeen* magazine open beside her.

"Don't *ever open my door* without knocking. What do you want?"

"May Jo wear your old tutu? We want to see how she'll look when she's a ballerina."

"OK, but knock next time. It's in the attic and you'd better put it back *or else*."

"Ya, ya." Laura gave her sister a dismissive look.

In the hallway she stood on a chair and pulled down a string attached to a door in the ceiling. A staircase slid down and we walked up into the attic. It was crowded with boxes and garment bags and smelled of mothballs. Laura took the light-blue tutu out of one of the bags.

Back in her room, I gingerly stepped into the tutu and carefully pulled it up.

"You look great! But it's a bit big. Turn around; I'll pin it in for you. There...have a look," Laura said, pointing at the floor-length mirror.

I looked at my body as I slowly turned around. My short blond hair and the tutu's sequins caught the afternoon sunlight. Miniature rainbows danced happily about the room. I smiled as I looked at my petite body. It hadn't begun to change. Some girls my age, like Laura, already wore bras. I contemplated my long legs and graceful arms. Perhaps I did have a dancer's body. For a moment, I forgot about my drooping eyelid.

"Oh, Laura, this tutu is fabulous! Let's put on some music and practice Mrs. Evans's new <u>combination</u>."

Laura pulled her long brown hair into a ponytail,

wiggled out of her slacks, and put on her light-pink tights, a leotard, and her ballet shoes. Then she placed a <u>ballet</u> <u>practice</u> <u>record</u> on her record player and we did some <u>grand pliés</u> to warm up our muscles.

"Saturday's combination was <u>glissade</u>, <u>jeté</u>, jeté, <u>changement</u>," I said, pleased that I'd remembered it.

Although Laura was smart, she didn't always remember the French names for the ballet steps or how to do them. Her long, lanky body made coordinating her movements difficult. So, I often helped her, as I did then, by demonstrating.

After practicing for over an hour, Laura wanted to stop. I was urging her to continue when the phone rang. I heard Mrs. Hardy's muffled voice downstairs.

"Jo," she yelled. "Your mother called. Something's

come up so she'll be picking you up in five minutes."

"OK," I yelled back, tugging the tutu off. I was putting on my clothes when Laura rushed out of the room. She came back with a jar of cold cream and a tissue.

"Oh, yikes, I forgot about the makeup!" I was wiping it off when I heard our car's horn.

"Don't panic. You've got all the makeup off. Your mom will never know!" said Laura, a sly look on her face.

I snatched up my jacket, pounded down the stairs, opened the door and turned around. "See you before class," I said. "I'll let you know if Mom notices any makeup."

"OK, but she won't. See you tomorrow."

The Surprise

The next day I met Laura outside the Durham Grange Hall or the Grange as we called it. "Did your mom see any makeup?" she asked.

"No, *thank goodness*. Come on. Let's go in," I said.

As we entered, I smelled the familiar scent of gas from the old stove in the kitchen. A short, narrow entryway served as a waiting room with a bench and bulletin board. I opened the next door to a large room where Mrs. Evans's younger students were ending their class. Along the walls were wooden chairs where we put our dance bags and jackets. At the front of the room, in the left corner, was a battered-looking, upright piano that Mrs. Prebble played for us. There were no mirrors. Every week Mrs. Evans set up chairs for us to use as our <u>barre</u>. We pushed them out of the way for our <u>center-floor</u> work. That's when we practiced dance combinations. Next, we danced diagonally from one corner of the room to the other doing leap and turns. Lastly there was <u>revérénce</u> to end our class. This was when we curtsied to a pretend audience and then to Mrs. Evans.

While the younger children were leaving, we put on our ballet shoes and waited until Mrs. Evans gathered us together. She was exotic-looking and appeared to be from another time, the eighteenth century perhaps, or from another country, possibly Spain. Her slick black hair was tied in a bun that rested, in a hairnet, at the back of her neck. Her blouses were long-sleeved with ruffled collars. She always wore an ankle-length, black skirt that stuck way out due to the many petticoats beneath it. Mrs. and Mr. Evans taught adults ballroom dancing and owned a farm where they had horses and hunting dogs. Mrs. Evans demanded respect and expected us to try our best. Her enthusiasm for dance was contagious.

Now, she said, "I am excited to tell you that the Boston Ballet Company will present the ballet *Alice in Wonderland* in Exeter this November." In my wildest dreams, I never imagined the Boston Ballet Company coming to Exeter, only two towns from Durham! "We'll be performing the 'Dance of the Playing Cards' with the company." Wow! I couldn't believe it. We'd be dancing on stage with *real ballet stars*. I felt my heart racing, my hands sweating. Mrs. Evans continued, "Next week after class I'll teach the first part of the dance. The following week we'll rehearse in Portsmouth with my advanced students. The third week we'll practice with costumes at the company's school. I will drive you to the rehearsals if your parents can't." My ballet dreams were becoming real! "I'll hand out a permission slip for your parents with information about the performance and rehearsal times at the end of class. Are there any questions?"

Several hands went up. Mrs. Evans called on Sally, a girl with long, brown braids and braces. "Who gets to dance Alice's part?"

"Fourteen-year-old Denise Collins, the <u>baby</u> <u>ballerina</u> of the Boston Ballet Company, is Alice. The company soloists will dance the leading roles like the White Rabbit and the Cheshire Cat. Children from the Boston Ballet School will dance in the Rose Garden Dance. Sorry our time is up. We must start class. If you have a question, speak with me after class. Mrs. Prebble, would you please find us some plié music?"

I quickly found an empty chair, placed my hand on its back and put my feet in <u>first</u> <u>position</u>. The music began and we started our pliés, slow knee-bending exercises. Next, we did our <u>tendus</u>, exercises to stretch and point our feet. Mrs. Evans reminded us to keep our heads up and feel what our feet were doing. But I looked down at the pattern my feet made rubbing against the dirty wooden floor. We progressed through a series of barre warmups ending with <u>grand</u> <u>battements</u> – my favorite, big leg kicks to the front, side and back.

It was hard concentrating on the center-floor work. I began to imagine twirling and jumping as a playing card. Somehow I managed to focus enough to get all the combinations correct. While doing our leaps across the floor, I saw myself wearing a bright red tutu with a white leotard on which were painted red hearts. I felt like I was suspended in the air, as if I were flying. My daydreaming was abruptly interrupted by the music for révérence. Then, as we were preparing to leave, Mrs. Evans handed out the permission slips and said, "See you next week."

I stuffed mine into my dance bag and grabbed my jacket. Then, smiling at Laura, we raced for the door. Outside the crisp fall air felt refreshing against my face. "I'm sure my mom will let me perform," I stated.

"Mine, too."

"I can't believe how lucky we are...actually dancing with professionals in the Boston Ballet Company! This is *the best* surprise," I said enthusiastically. "Perhaps when we rehearse *Alice in Wonderland*, the <u>ballet</u> <u>mistress</u> will ask us to join the Boston Ballet School."

"Highly unlikely, but, if she did, how would we get there? Boston is at least an hour and a half ride each way and our parents aren't going to drive us."

"I don't know. Maybe we could ride the bus to Boston and take classes in the city on Saturdays."

"Our mothers would never let us take the bus alone."

"You're right. Someday, though, when I'm older, I'll take the bus and dance with the Boston Ballet School on Saturdays. Wait and see," I announced with conviction. "I hate living so far from Boston. City kids take ballet classes every day. How are we ever going to compete with them when we take only one class a week?" I moaned.

"Who knows? Right now all I care about is having something to eat. I'm starved. I hope there's something good in the fridge. Give me a call and let me know if your mom approves," Laura said, heading toward her parents' car.

"Will do." I waved goodbye.

I skipped all the way home, excitement racing through me like a powerful river rushing downstream. I burst into the kitchen where Mom was sorting laundry.

"Mom, Mom, guess what?! Our class is performing with the Boston Ballet in *Alice in Wonderland* this November. We're going to be the playing cards. Isn't that great?! Here, read this." I thrust the permission slip into her hand. "Can I do it? Please, please?"

Mom read the notice. "Sounds terrific, Honey."

"You mean I've got your permission?"

"For sure!" Mom replied, unable to hide her enthusiasm. "This is a wonderful opportunity."

"Oh, Mom, you're the best." I gave her a quick hug around the waist, and then flew to the phone.

"Hi, Laura? I can perform. Can you?"

"Yup, my mom agreed right away."

"Wonderful! I can't wait till Saturday's rehearsal."

"Me either. Bye, Jo."

Leslie Louise

The next Saturday, after our class, Mrs. Evans collected permission slips, money, and then counted the girls. "Eight. That's perfect; this is a partner dance."

Laura and I turned to each other and grabbed hands. "Can we be partners, Mrs. Evans?" Laura begged. "Please."

"Oh, you two, I should have known. You're like two peas in a pod! Well, OK."

Mrs. Evans assigned the other partners and instructed everyone to line up.

"You girls will be the leaders." She nodded to Laura and me. "We'll start here, at the back of an imaginary stage. Pretend the curtain opened. March with your partner down center stage almost to the front edge of the stage where you'll move apart slightly. Girls on stage right, put your right foot front. Girls on stage left do the opposite. Then do two tendus to the side closing back, two changements, two jetés and repeat. Make all your steps small or your costume will be hitting you."

The first part of the dance went well but the rest of it presented a challenge. Everyone moved simultaneously to different places on the pretend stage. Although the steps were easy, remembering our places proved tricky. Next, we posed for twenty-four counts, imagining the

Portsmouth students dancing their part.

Some girls complained that the dance was confusing. Mrs. Evans stopped us to explain. "Mrs. Ashford's <u>choreography</u> is different from mine. Professional dancers must frequently learn new choreography, which takes them time, too. The dance will come together when we rehearse with my Portsmouth students. Until then, try to remember the steps, your places and your poses. Ballerinas need excellent memories. Let's end for today."

❧

On Wednesday, Mrs. Evans drove us to the Ballard Center for the Arts in Portsmouth, New Hampshire. The rehearsal space was a glassed-in porch that overlooked the last of the fall flowers. Sitting on the floor stretching her legs was a dancer with a freckled face and a bright red ponytail.

"Hello," I said, walking around her outstretched legs. She kept reaching toward her pointed toes. I wondered if she'd heard me. I plunked my coat down on an empty chair and picked up my dance bag when the redhead snapped, "Hey! That's my chair. Get your own."

"I didn't know it was *your chair*," I protested, stunned by her attitude.

"My shoes are under it. Didn't you see them?"

"No, I didn't," I replied.

"What's wrong with your eye anyway?"

I couldn't believe her lack of tact.

"That's none of your business," I snapped back.

"Come on, Jo; bring your coat over here. We'll share this chair," Laura said with disdain. On the way to the dressing room she was fuming. "Miss Redhead thinks she's a <u>prima ballerina</u>, doesn't she?"

"You can say that again!"

The ladies' lounge of the Ballard Center contained a dressing room that smelled of stale perfume. Inside four Portsmouth girls fixed their hair and changed their clothes. They greeted us pleasantly.

When we returned, Mrs. Evans had us form a circle and introduce ourselves. The redhead was last. "I'm Leslie Louise Marren. I'm called Leslie Louise, not just Leslie," she announced. Her ponytail whipped proudly back and forth like the tail of a circus horse.

Mrs. Evans asked her Portsmouth dancers to line up, which they did like obedient toy soldiers. Then she positioned us on the imaginary stage and started the music. The dance started off well, but, after I separated from Laura, I crashed into Leslie Louise.

"You're in my spot!" screamed Leslie Louise. "Mrs. Evans, she's taken my spot."

Mrs. Evans stopped the music and hurriedly thumbed through her notebook.

"I am supposed to stop here," I insisted.

"Girls, girls, calm down. Let me see. Jo, move to your left a bit. Good, that's where you'll pose."

After Mrs. Evans walked away, Leslie Louise hissed, "Wake up, Stupid."

I whispered back, "I am *not* stupid. Don't call me that." I wanted to call her a miserable, mean-spirited witch but I glared at her instead.

After the rehearsal, Mrs. Evans discussed Saturday afternoon's rehearsal in Harwich. "Miss Lawton, the ballet mistress, will teach us the last part of the dance and explain where it fits into the whole ballet. We've done enough for today. If you're going home with me, be ready to leave in ten minutes."

On the ride home, I whispered into Laura's ear, "*I can't stand Leslie Louise!*"

The Boston Rehearsal

It was raining heavily as Mrs. Evans's car headed for Boston and, to make matters worse, she had forgotten her glasses. She was nearly blind without them. So, Laura, two other girls in our class, and I attempted to read the highway signs for her.

"Boston Back Bay, Exit 4, next right," Laura exclaimed.

The car swerved and skidded to the right, tossing up a spray of water from the highway. I gripped the front seat.

Gradually I relaxed as we drove along the Charles River, watching the skyscrapers of Boston emerge from the fog. Off the highway, we were greeted by a subway trolley screeching along its above-ground tracks. People carrying umbrellas dodged frantically around cars, trucks, and numerous puddles.

Finally, we arrived at the Boston Ballet School, located on the second floor of an enormous brick building on a busy avenue. Miss Lawton, a wiry little lady with grey hair, a pointed chin and pleasant smile, greeted Mrs. Evans. Then, turning to us, she said, "Welcome, girls, the dressing room is next door. Get dressed quickly and go down the hall to studio two. The studio is only available for an hour and a half. So, make it snappy."

I was putting on my leotard and tights in the small dark dressing room when Laura tapped my shoulder. Whispering into my ear, she said, "Guess who just arrived."

"No doubt it's Lousy Leslie Louise, prima ballerina," I whispered back, surprised by my own rudeness. Ordinarily, I wasn't so catty.

After dressing, we walked past a small office full of dancers to studio two. It was a large, shabby-looking room with a well-worn wooden floor and paint peeling from the walls. Two men in white tee shirts, black tights and black ballet shoes finished practicing some leaps. A ballerina sat on the floor unlacing her toe shoes. There was a baby grand piano in one corner piled high with sheet music and dirty coffee cups full of old cigarette butts.

Odd, I mused, to see ballerinas dressed in old warm-up clothes, dancing in grungy rooms, smoking cigarettes. It didn't fit my picture of a ballerina's life. Once the dancers left the room, Mrs. Evans and Miss Lawton began positioning dancers. I hurried to my spot. Then, when everyone was ready, we rehearsed the dance.

"Very good, very good," praised Miss Lawton, rapidly clapping her hands. "Now we'll learn the end of the dance." She demonstrated the steps only once and expected us to remember them. The Portsmouth dancers had no problem so Miss Lawton continued, "Alright, we'll go on."

Go on? I didn't remember the steps she'd just taught. I stole a glance at Laura. She struggled to keep up, too.

I remembered Mrs. Evans's advice. Be patient; new choreography took time to learn. But I wanted to do it perfectly *now*.

"Stop, stop!" demanded Miss Lawton in a very loud voice. "Girls, move to the back if you don't know the choreography. We can't waste time. You with the red hair and you in the purple leotard, come front. You'll be my leaders. Quickly, girls. Move!"

Laura and I moved to the back. I learned the choreography after several repetitions. However, Laura appeared completely confused.

After rehearsing the ending a few more times, Miss Lawton read names for costume fittings. I was among the first group of girls but not Laura. We followed Mrs. Evans to the costume room, which smelled like a musty old attic. Boxes and trunks of all sizes were stacked from floor to ceiling and several large sewing machines filled the middle of the room. Two racks of costumes, stuffed full of long sheer skirts, tutus and capes of all colors, shapes and sizes lined the sides of the room. In a corner sat a stack of sandwich boards designed just like playing cards, made of two pieces of cardboard, one for the front and one for the back, attached with cloth shoulder straps. Mrs. Evans placed a sandwich board over the girl ahead of me. It covered her from chest to knees! Now I understood why our movements needed to be small. My sandwich board perfectly replicated a five-of-hearts playing card. Fortunately, I left the costume room without hitting myself, anything, or anyone.

When I returned to studio two, Leslie Louise was

demonstrating the new choreography for Laura. I overheard her thanking Leslie Louise as they left for their costumes. My cheeks grew hot. My pulse raced. Anger gripped me.

With everyone in costume, Miss Lawton had us re-hearse the entire dance. Even using smaller steps, my costume kept hitting my knees. I looked down for a mi-nute. Wham, my sandwich board crashed into Leslie Louise's.

"Watch out, Bonehead! You nearly knocked me over."

The music stopped. "There is *no talking*, dancers," Miss Lawton ordered. "Pay attention or we'll have a real accident." She stared right at me! My stomach felt queasy. It seemed like an eternity before she spoke. "OK, take it from the top again."

I wondered what that meant until I saw everyone moving to their places for the beginning of the dance. This time, I completed the dance, much to my relief, without hitting myself or anyone else.

"Well done, girls," praised Miss Lawton. "Overall, you were quite patient with these awkward costumes. Now that you're used to them, I'm sure we won't have any more collisions. Practice the choreography several times during the next week. Remember to replay it in your mind's eye. In other words, think through the dance without doing it. Please be careful when you re-stack your costumes. See you in Exeter for the dress re-hearsal very soon."

Leslie Louise was the first dancer to thank Miss Law-ton. When it was my turn, I nervously stuttered my thanks. Miss Lawton's face broke into a wide smile. She bent down and whispered, "I know you won't let that miserable old costume get in your way again."

Surprising myself, I look right at her warm blue eyes and confidently whispered back, "No way!"

I lost Laura during the confusion in the costume room but, a few minutes later, I froze at the doorway of the dressing room where I heard her exchanging phone numbers with Leslie Louise. I felt as if Laura had slapped me across my face. We were best friends, weren't we? I wanted to scream. Instead, I turned away, changed into my street clothes and waited in the hallway, fuming.

I walked over to Laura after Leslie Louise had left with the Portsmouth dancers. Attempting to sound nonchalant, I asked, "Why did you take Leslie Louise's phone number?"

"Well," she paused, trying to find the right words, "she's got something special to tell me. That's all."

"I see. It's a secret. Thanks a lot. I thought you hated Leslie Louise."

"She's really not that bad once you get to know her. You're getting worked up over nothing, Jo."

I wanted to refute her words, but my throat tightened up. I said nothing. I knew my voice would crack if I did. We met Mrs. Evans, left the ballet studio and rode home in silence.

The Performance

The night of the rehearsal, Laura and I walked through the Exeter, New Hampshire High School gymnasium, a large room with a poorly-maintained stage at its end. Metal folding chairs were arranged in rows for the audience. We walked up the stairs to the stage where Mrs. Evans's dancers warmed up doing pliés. Other dancers stood in groups talking or sitting on the floor stretching their legs.

Soon Mrs. Ashford, the creative director of the Boston Ballet Company, arrived. A tall woman in a flowered dress and high heels, she marched with authority to the center of the stage and summoned everyone: members of the Boston Ballet Company, dancers from the Boston Ballet School and Mrs. Evans's students.

"OK, let's begin," she announced, in a harsh, business-like tone. "We'll run through the show twice. First, we'll do the stage lighting and music cues with the first-act dancers. Second-act dancers, you will sit in the audience to watch the first-act. There will be *total silence.*" Mrs. Ashford glared in our direction. "Is that understood? Good. Then, second-act dancers will be called. During the last run-though, there's no stopping. Second-act dancers will wait in the backstage dressing area. First-act dancers take your places; the first run-through begins in five minutes."

Mrs. Evans ushered us to the front row of chairs. Laura motioned for Leslie Louise to sit with us. I felt a chill. This was the last thing I wanted. The lights dimmed and the music began. As the curtain opened, the White Rabbit appeared. The man dancing the part wore a large rabbit-head made of papier-mâché, a blue vest and a red plaid jacket. He jumped about the stage, stopping often to look at his pocket watch. Alice, sitting in the corner, looked up, startled by him. She wore a white pinafore over a light-blue dress. Her blonde hair hung in loose golden curls around her shoulders. Suddenly, she was twirling rapidly after the White Rabbit on her toe shoes.

"Look, there's Denise Collins. Isn't she beautiful!" whispered Leslie Louise to Laura.

Laura leaned over to her, whispered something back and gave her a quick hug. I felt as if a door had been slammed in my face. Hatred, like red-hot coals, burned through me. Attempting to calm down, I focused on Alice as she danced offstage after the White Rabbit. Suddenly, the stage went dark and I heard a soft swishing sound. When the lights returned, Alice danced on to the stage in front of a backdrop on which a row of different-sized doors was painted.

Suddenly, Mrs. Ashford yelled, "Stop!" Then, facing the back of the gymnasium where the lighting crew and music were set up, she hollered, "Stop the music! Keep the stage totally dark until Alice reappears. Put the spotlight on her while the stagehands move the table onto the stage. Only then bring the lights up. We'll take it from where Alice enters. Music, please."

Alice leapt around the stage with the spotlight following her. She stopped now and then, looking for the White Rabbit. The lights went up as planned revealing a three-legged table with a key on it. Mrs. Ashford stopped the music again. "Add more orange light near the table. Up a bit more. Yes, that's it, good."

The ballet continued with Mrs. Ashford stopping the rehearsal at each scene to direct the lighting crew or stagehands. I grew impatient. When would we dance? Do all dress rehearsals take this long? Probably they do, I reasoned, and, if so, professional dancers must wait a long time during dress rehearsals.

Finally, second-act dancers were called. Backstage, we put on our costumes and lined up. Everyone moved carefully around the stagehands and the ropes hanging from the ceiling that were pulled to change backdrops. My heart pounding, we took our places in the <u>wings</u>. Soon the Playing Card Dance music began and we were on stage!

The rest of the first run-through required only minor adjustments to the lighting and the second run-through went smoothly. Afterwards, while returning our costumes, Laura stopped me. "I don't need a ride home with you tomorrow."

"Oh? How come?" Mom planned to take her home after the performance because Laura's parents had another commitment.

Laura looked around the backstage, avoiding eye

contact. "I'm staying overnight at Leslie Louise's. Her mom will drive us."

"You're spending the night with *her*?" I eyed her with disbelief.

"I know you're not crazy about Leslie Louise, Jo, but you really haven't given her a chance."

"Given her a chance! That's a joke."

"No, I mean it. Someday you might even like her." She attempted a weak smile.

"Highly unlikely."

"Well, we're still friends, aren't we?" she asked with trepidation.

"Ya, I guess so but why do you like Leslie Louise when she's so mean to me?"

"She's...how can I say it? She's worldly. You know, grown up."

"Right! Tell me another." I was almost shouting. Suddenly, I wanted to flee the backstage, but, before I did, I had to speak up. "Leslie Louise is an arrogant, mean-spirited girl. You're stupid for being friends with her."

Stunned, Laura just stared at me, so I spun around and left.

᠙ᕇᕒ

The next night, I noticed Leslie Louise and Laura leaving Denise's backstage dressing area. They were clutching a bag. Laura caught my eye but turned away. She and Leslie Louise rushed off giggling and jumping about, ignoring me as if I were invisible.

They were up to something, but I forced myself to focus on getting my costume and preparing for the show.

The performance started. Soon the Playing Card Dance began. Everything went well until halfway through it when I felt my right shoe strap snap off. As I danced, the shoe grew looser and looser. Then, with one kick it went sliding across the stage like a hockey puck on an ice rink. My face felt burning-hot. The shoe landed in the middle of the stage and I was dancing with one shoe on, one shoe off. What a fool! Why hadn't I checked my elastic shoe strap before the performance? I struggled to hold back tears. I moved mechanically through the rest of the dance. Once offstage, I immediately burst into tears. Mrs. Evans rushed over.

"I'm so embarrassed," I cried, brushing the tears from my face.

"I know. But you did the right thing by continuing to dance as if nothing had happened. You didn't miss a step. Losing your shoe could have easily distracted you."

"Really?" In my mind's eye, I looked ridiculous clomping about the stage wearing only one shoe.

"Yes. You didn't lose your place or confuse the other dancers."

I hadn't thought of that. I'd kept dancing because I didn't know what else to do.

Mrs. Evans continued, "Chalk it up to experience. You never know what could go wrong during a performance. From now on, you'll check the elastic straps on your shoes to be sure they are sewed on tightly. Now, go get this awkward costume off," she said, and left to talk with Mrs. Ashford.

I headed to Miss Lawton who was helping the others remove their sandwich boards and stacking them on a dolly. There, I saw Stacey, a dancer from my class, in line ahead of me. After Miss Lawton removed her costume, she ran away and returned shortly with my shoe.

"Sorry about your shoe, Jo. Here it is. I saw one of the dancers kick it backstage."

"Thanks," I said, too self-conscious to look at her.

We headed for the dressing room together. I was grateful for her silence. She knew I wasn't in the mood to talk. I wanted to vanish when I saw Leslie Louise and Laura ahead of us.

"Poor thing!" Leslie Louise said in a loud voice. "She can't even keep her shoes on!" They looked at each other, burst into laughter and bounded off.

Losing my shoe was humiliating enough without their rudeness. Stacey tried to comfort me, but I turned away, covering my face with my hands.

I changed into my dress, scooped up my dance bag and found my parents waiting in the auditorium. Mom had a bouquet of flowers for me. Dad had his camera.

"Why the sad face?" Mom asked.

"It's pretty obvious isn't it?" I blurted out.

"What are you talking about?" she demanded.

"Didn't you see me dancing with one shoe on and one shoe off? The strap on my ballet shoe broke off. I lost my shoe in the middle of the dance."

"You did? I didn't notice. Did you, John?" she asked, turning to Dad.

"No. We never knew. The stage lights on the floor, at the front of the stage, hid your feet. Besides, you looked confident up there," he added.

"Seriously?"

"Seriously. Now where's your beautiful smile? I want a picture of my ballerina before we leave."

I forced myself to smile as the camera flashed.

Then Mom asked, "Hey, Jo, where's Laura? Isn't she coming with us?"

"Oh...I forgot to tell you. She's staying overnight with Leslie Louise."

"OK," she said. Her look revealed concern. "Well, let's go home then."

❧

Laura called the next night, Sunday, with a question about an after-school event. I ignored her question. Confronting her instead, I asked, "Why'd you laugh at me yesterday? I thought we were best friends."

"Oh, don't take it so seriously. It was just hysterical watching you dance with only one shoe."

"Real funny. Ha, ha."

Laura's tone of voice softened, "Come on, Jo," she pleaded. "Let's forget it. I'm sorry...OK?"

Maybe she regretted hurting me. Could I forgive her? I waited before responding. "We'll see," I said with mixed emotions.

The New Students

During December Laura and I resumed our friendship, though tentatively on my part. Then, one day after Christmas vacation, I stopped dead in my tracks. When Laura and I entered the Grange there, to my horror, was Leslie Louise. Now what would become of Laura and my friendship?

She rushed over to Leslie Louise like I assumed she would. "What are you doing here?"

"My mom says I need three to four classes a week if I'm going to be a professional ballerina. I've got to be *the best* to get into a company. So, I'll be taking this class every Saturday and classes at the Boston Ballet School during the week."

"That's terrific news!" said Laura, smiling. "Your mom's the best."

"I think so." Leslie Louise's face lit up; she tossed her ponytail about and smiled.

Mrs. Marren, a heavy-set woman with a round face and a loud voice, was talking to Mrs. Evans. I remembered her. She'd been at all the rehearsals, watching us with her unfriendly eyes. Once Mrs. Marren found a seat, Mrs. Evans gathered us around her. She introduced Leslie Louise to the girls who hadn't been in the performance and began the class.

We warmed up at the barre, and then moved to our places for the center floor work. Leslie Louise placed herself in the front row, puffed out her chest and stuck her chin in the air. The first combination was very slow requiring a lot of leg strength. Leslie Louise's arabesque was perfect. My leg quivered from the strain. Later, doing turns across the floor, she turned rapidly with a confident step and a snap of her head. My turns looked pathetic in comparison. I turned slowly and deliberately. *Someday*, I thought, *my turns are going to be just as good...even better.* As the class ended, I knew I was no longer the best in the class. It felt like I'd been hit in my gut.

After Leslie Louise and her mother left, Laura said, "You'll never believe Leslie Louise's and my secret. Promise not to tell?"

"Promise."

"Remember when we were in the *Alice in Wonderland* Ballet? Well, Leslie Louise and I met Denise Collins backstage where she gave us a pair of her toe shoes. She signed her name and wrote on them for us. She wished us good luck with our ballet careers. At Leslie Louise's house, we took turns stuffing tissues into the toe shoes and dancing <u>on</u> <u>pointe</u>. It really felt weird. I had trouble staying up, wobbling like crazy. When Leslie Louise tried on Denise's toe shoes, she wasn't as wobbly."

"Oh," was all I said. Images of Leslie Louise and Laura trying on the toe shoes, laughing and having fun, made me so jealous and angry that I was sure it showed on my face.

Laura, however, continued totally unaware of my emotions. "It felt kind of strange going up on my toes, but I didn't care. I felt like a *real* ballerina! Before I went home, we decided Leslie Louise should keep the toe shoes because her mother had arranged for us to see Denise Collins. But, now that Leslie Louise is taking the Saturday class, we're going to share them. She'll bring the toe shoes next week. Then, I'll keep them for two weeks. Want to borrow them next Saturday for a week?"

Mrs. Hardy had arrived and was honking her car horn.

"Maybe," I yelled after her as she rushed to her mom.

Walking home, I thought about having my own pair of signed toe shoes and how it would feel to be on pointe. That afternoon I had an idea. I took a piece of notepaper and wrote, *Wanted: one pair of signed, used toe shoes. Call 928-2235.* I knew it was a far-fetched plan but maybe, just maybe, someone in the class would have a relative who was a ballerina. Then, I folded the notice and tucked it into my school bag.

A few days later, on my way home from school, I headed for the Grange to post my notice. I was in luck. The building was open. A group of women were preparing for a Grange dinner. I tacked my notice on the bulletin board in the entryway. The thought of getting a used pair of toe shoes was so exciting that I could hardly wait for my next ballet class.

When Saturday arrived, I noticed a new girl, who I thought was Chinese, speaking with Mrs. Evans as the younger students were leaving. Slightly taller than me, she had a strikingly beautiful appearance, dark brown almond-shaped eyes and shiny black hair worn in a bun. She had a petite body, long legs and moved with the graceful confidence of a ballerina. I guessed that she was eighteen years old or older.

Before our class started, Mrs. Evans introduced her. "This is Allison Ming. She has just moved here from San Francisco, California where she studied with the West Coast Ballet Academy. She's had two years of pointe class and has performed in several of their ballets. Allison's a sophomore at Oyster River High School and I've asked her to assist me with both of my classes." Mrs. Evans had us introduce ourselves, and then said, "By-the-way, someone left a notice on the bulletin board looking for a pair of used toe shoes."

Oh, no, I thought. *Please* don't ask who wrote the notice.

Mrs. Evans continued, "It's fine to have someone else's toe shoes but wearing them isn't safe. Toe shoes must be specially fitted to each dancer. You can hurt yourself by wearing toe shoes that aren't yours and don't fit correctly. OK, let's begin class." I sighed with relief. Laura wouldn't know I'd written the notice.

Although our class was harder than usual, watching Allison was inspirational. She seemed to become one with the music, flying along its high notes, twirling and leaping, her body singing. Somehow, watching her dance gave me new energy. Soon nothing mattered but the music and my dancing! In my excitement, I forgot all about Leslie Louise until after class when she and Laura approached me.

"You, jerk! You *promised* not to tell anyone about the toe shoes," hissed Laura.

"I didn't *tell* anyone."

"But that was *your notice*. Wasn't it? You wanted your own pair. Well, good luck with that! Now, I'm not letting you borrow Denise Collins's toe shoes," she announced, taking them from Leslie Louise and quickly tucking them into her dance bag. Together they walked out the door.

At the bulletin board, I ripped down my notice and sank onto a bench. Laura's words left me feeling angry and alone. I stared off into space.

"Were you the one looking for used toe shoes?" asked Allison. She had changed into her street clothes and let her hair down, which made her look younger. She was about to leave.

"Yes," I confessed.

"I overheard your friends saying they won't share their pair."

"That's right," I mumbled.

"Would you like a pair of my old toe shoes?"

"Are you kidding?" I looked at her in disbelief. She didn't even know me.

"No, I'm not kidding! I'll be here next Saturday. You can get them then, if you want. This is our secret. OK?"

I smiled up at her. "OK. Thanks a lot. See you then."

One-Eye

Monday was cold and grey as I walked into school and upstairs to my homeroom. As usual, Laura was waiting outside the door. She looked upset.

"What's the matter, Laura?"

"I've got something difficult to say." She paused and looked down at her hands for a very long time. "I'm not talking with you during school or by phone."

"What? How come?"

"Leslie Louise says you're not pretty and my other friends agree. So, I've decided...We're not friends anymore."

I stared at her. Holding back tears, I yelled, "You're a jerk, Laura Hardy, a real lousy jerk. You're not my friend either. *So there.* Someday you'll regret this, I promise."

I flew down the stairs and outside toward home. It had started to snow. Tiny snowflakes, like knives, stabbed my face. Tears fell against the hard, cold pavement as I ran.

I hated it. I just hated it. Why did I have to be born with a drooping eyelid? Nobody's eyes were as ugly. I hated it. Hated, *hated, hated it!*

At home, I rushed to my room, slammed the door and locked it.

"What's wrong, Sweetheart?" called my mom through the door.

"Nothing. *Leave me alone,*" I cried.

I could hear Mom rattling the door handle. "Open this door! Tell me what happened. Why aren't you in school? Are you sick?"

"Go away. Just go *away!*" I hollered.

"Jo...Jo, answer me."

I refused. Instead, I flung myself onto my bed. A black wall of despair wrapped around me. I heard my mother insistently knocking on the door, each knock pounding my head. Finally, it stopped. I sank deeper into blackness. I was *never* going back to dance, not with Leslie Louise and Laura there. I couldn't. Pain clutched my stomach. I felt like I was about to throw up. I thrust my face deeper into my pillow. How could Laura be so mean? All she cared about was having pretty, popular friends. I swore I'd get even with her somehow; I just didn't know how yet. My head ached. My eyes stung. A deep exhaustion swept over me. I must have fallen asleep because the next thing I heard was my dad's voice.

"Jo, open this door immediately!" he demanded. "Your mother and I want to talk with you."

I couldn't say "no" to Dad. He rarely got upset but when he did, there was no disobeying. I slid off the bed, unlocked the door and gingerly opened it. His kind face showed deep lines of worry.

"What's this all about?" he asked, as he led me to the living room where he sat on the sofa with Mom.

I began to cry. Big tears splashed onto my sweater. "Laura refuses to talk with me 'cause she wants to be popular. Popular girls are beautiful. She says I'm not grown-up or pretty. So, we're not friends anymore," I stammered.

"Oh," he said, slowly reflecting on what I'd said. "I see...come over here. Sit beside me." He encircled me with his big, sturdy arms, then gently cupped my chin and lifted my head. "It's not the way your face looks that determines your beauty. You're special, Jo, beautiful just because you're you."

Suddenly I felt anger boiling inside me, anger I'd never expressed. "Sure, Dad, you can say that because your eyelids are normal. People don't gawk at you, always asking about what happened to your eye?' I am *so sick* of it." I leapt off the sofa, gathered my courage and shouted, the words exploding from my mouth, "I HATE YOU! You didn't fix my birth defect. My face is *ugly*. No wonder I have no friends. I really, really HATE you."

No one spoke. I stood before my parents, staring right at them, refusing to cry.

Finally, Mom broke the silence. She would normally chastise me for being rude. Instead, she spoke so softly I hardly heard her. "We would do anything to fix your eyelid if we could, Sweetheart, but there are some things you can't change in life. We took you to the best hospital. Boston's Children's Hospital is world-renowned for its eye surgery department. Nothing more can be done."

I knew this. Dr. Gunderson, a famous Boston eye

surgeon, tried to surgically lift my paralyzed left eyelid. I'd had the operation when I was five, but my eyelid failed to rise more than halfway. Dr. Gunderson had explained that another operation would be too dangerous; I could lose my eye.

Mom continued, "We know how terribly upsetting it is for you to look different."

"No you don't," I shot back. How could she possibly know?

"Remember your father's words," Mom said, ignoring my outburst. "And, don't let what others say or do bother you."

Her calm attitude amazed and irritated me. "That's easy for you to say, Mom." A fire burned in my stomach. "Just how do I ignore other people? Pretend I am invisible? What do you suggest?" I didn't wait for an answer. "NOTHING!"

"Pull yourself together, Jo. It's not the end of the world. There are a lot of worse things," Mom insisted.

"Yeah, sure," I responded, my voice ripe with sarcasm. I immediately swirled around and left the room, my feet pounding the floor. My heart beat so loudly that I hardly heard Dad calling my name. I slammed my bedroom door really hard, as if to say end of discussion. Exhausted, I flopped onto my bed. As my heart rate slowed, I heard my parent's muffled voices arguing. I crept to the door, pressing my ear against it.

"Maybe we should have had that second opinion, or at least seen the New York City ophthalmologist your mother mentioned when Jo was a baby."

"Stop rehashing things, John. Dr. Gunderson was the better surgeon. He did the best he could." Mom's voice rose.

"Jo's obviously in enormous emotional pain, Maryanna. Can't you see that?" Dad asked.

"Of course I see it. Believe me; I feel her pain. What do you think?" Mom was almost screaming. "Look, she's a strong, resilient child, John. I believe she won't remain a victim of this. She'll get through it; we'll all get through it."

Nothing seemed clear. Should they have taken me to the other doctor? Would his surgery have worked? Why hadn't they consulted him? What good was it now? Why did Mom say that I was strong? Was she just appeasing Dad? What did being strong have to do with being accepted or not? My mind felt like a top spinning out of control. I moved away from the door.

Strangely, Mom's words kept coming back. "She's a strong, resilient child." Was I? I clung to her words as if I were clinging to the edge of a cliff.

❧

I was miserable the rest of the week. At school, during recess, Laura and her popular friends kept looking at me, turning away and whispering. I stood alone staring at the ground, kicking the dirt. It was a huge relief when the recess bell rang.

On Saturday, a little before ten o'clock, Mom came to my door, a distressed look in her eyes. "It's time you left

for ballet. Why aren't you ready?"

"I'm *not* going," I insisted.

"What?"

"I said *I'm not going.*"

"Get dressed this minute. I'll drive you."

"But..."

"But nothing. Get moving."

I turned to face her but she'd left. I grabbed my tights, tugged fiercely to pull them up, threw on a leotard and headed for the car.

At the Grange, I found Laura and Leslie Louise in the entryway fixing each other's hair. They didn't notice me as I rushed past them. I was putting on my ballet shoes

when I saw Allison leaving. I found a chair just as the class began. During the center floor, I fumbled my way through it, ignoring Laura and Leslie Louise as much as possible.

After révérence, Mrs. Evans gathered us around her. "I have more exciting information for you! Yesterday, I received a flyer from the Boston Ballet. The company is holding auditions at the Old Opera House in Boston on Sunday, February sixteenth for a "Stars and Stripes" <u>solo</u> in their May performance. Madame Petrova, the former ballerina of the Bolshoi Ballet in Russia, will give the audition. Mrs. Ashford, Miss Lawton and Mr. Arthur Mitchell, a principal male dancer from the New York City Ballet, will be the judges. They will evaluate dancers on their ballet technique and artistic expression. Raise your hand if you're interested in trying out for the audition." Everyone, except me, raised their hand. Mrs. Evans continued, "Remember, your parents have to give you permission and arrange for your transportation. I've left a pile of permission slips in the entryway; take one before you leave. You must return it within the next two weeks."

On my way out, Mrs. Evans stopped me. She gave me a warm smile and handed me a Capezio toe shoe box. "Allison left this for you. She couldn't stay for your class today."

"Oh, thank you," I said. I'd forgotten about Allison's toe shoes.

"I didn't see your hand go up. You're getting stronger and beginning to show real ballerina potential. I hope you're planning to audition."

I was taken aback. Did she mean it? I wondered. "I might. Do you seriously think I have a chance?"

"You never know, Jo, but I have every confidence in you. You're always striving to do your best, so, even if you aren't chosen, it's a great experience. Ballerinas attend lots of auditions during their careers. For example, they audition to join a company or to get a particular part in a ballet. So, ballet dancers must get used to auditioning."

Maybe I should audition. I don't want to give up simply because of Laura's nasty comment. Auditioning would be interesting and exciting, I thought, as I put Allison's toe shoe box into my dance bag and donned

my winter coat. I grabbed a permission slip before I
left.

Outside, beside the Grange, a snowplow had formed
a huge pile of snow crusted over with ice. Laura and
three other girls from class knelt behind it. Suddenly,
ice balls flew like miniature rockets by me. *Smack.* An
ice ball hit my left eye. Cold, stinging pain mixed with
my hot tears.

"See you later, One-Eye. Bye-bye, One-Eye. Bye-bye,
One-Eye, One-Eye, One-Eye," they yelled as they ran
away.

I lay in a heap on the snow. Pieces of ice and dirt
streaked down my face. I grew wetter and colder. I
didn't care. *Nobody in ballet class likes me*, I thought,
gasping for air. I wanted to stay there and freeze but my
eye began to throb. Reluctantly, I got up, picked up the
wet permission slip and my dance bag. Bye-bye One-
Eye, One-Eye, One-Eye, ran through my mind as I
slowly trudged home.

The Diary

Luckily no one was home. I threw the wet notice on the kitchen table, fled to my room and dumped Allison's Capezio box on the floor by my bureau. What is the point of hanging Allison's toes shoes up? I'll return her shoes when I have the nerve to tell her I've quit ballet. Bleak despair returned. I lay on my bed most of the afternoon crying.

Finally, I got up, opened my bureau feverishly tossing leotards and tights onto the floor. Then I rummaged through my closet for a bag to contain them. Instead, I found the old, faded diary my grandfather had given me. Inside was his familiar handwriting.

To Jo, here is one of my empty diaries for you to fill with all the wonderful things about yourself and your life. With Love, Grampie

Suddenly, it felt like he was right beside me. I hugged the book close, and then I turned the page to an entry I'd written six months earlier.

Ballet is so wonderful! Today I know, I really know, that I am meant to be a ballerina. It's something deep inside of me. NO MATTER WHAT, I have to dance.

I turned the page and began to write.

Last week, Laura said she didn't want to be friends anymore because I am not pretty. All her popular, pretty friends agreed and ignored me. Today after ballet class, Laura and some other dancers threw snowballs at me and called me One-Eye. I wasn't going to let her nasty comments upset me but now I want to quit ballet. I can't take ANY MORE humiliation.

Writing helped me feel better. I closed the diary, hid it in a corner of my closet and shut the door. In front of me spread the abandoned pile of leotards and tights. I scooped them up and stuffed them back into my bureau, planning to throw them out in a few days.

That night, as we were cleaning the kitchen after dinner, Mom expressed concern. "Are you feeling alright, Jo? You've been in your room all day."

"I'm fine. Just fine. *Stop asking me.*"

"OK, but tell me about this notice," she said, holding up the crumpled permission slip.

"What's there to tell? It's just some dumb audition," I said, scrubbing the kitchen counter as hard as I could to avoid eye contact with her.

"Aren't you interested in trying out?" She sounded puzzled.

"I don't know. I doubt it." When I looked up, I could tell Mom was debating about what to say.

"Why not think about it? You don't have to decide for another week or so," she advised.

I turned away without answering.

ೋೋ

The Oyster River Junior and Senior High Schools were in the same building and used the same cafeteria. As the junior high students left the lunchroom, the high school students entered.

Several days later, Allison arrived in the cafeteria just as I was about to leave. She said, "How do you like my old toe shoes?"

"I love them! I hung them over my mirror where I see them every day." I hoped my smile concealed the discomfort I felt. Fortunately, Allison appeared to accept my lie without reservation.

"I'm glad. You're auditioning for the 'Stars and Stripes' solo, aren't you?"

"I guess so."

"What do you mean, you guess so?" Dismay registered on her face. "I'd love to audition but I'm over the age limit."

I began to speak, and then stopped, as I handed my empty food tray to the lunch lady. Allison walked with me to the cafeteria door. Before I left, I quietly said, "I'm considering quitting ballet." The words came out easier than I'd thought.

"No! Really? Why?"

I explained that it was personal, but I really wanted to tell her how much Laura and her friends had humiliated me.

"I could help you prepare for the audition. Mrs. Evans won't mind. I'll speak to her."

"*Wow, really*?" I never anticipated Allison's help.

"Sure. I'd love to help. You've got nothing to lose."

"You're right; there's nothing to lose," I said, a note of confidence returning to my voice.

"Good. Here." Allison wrote her phone number on a scrap of paper and handed it to me. "Give me a call tomorrow after I've spoken with Mrs. Evans."

"Thanks." I stuffed the paper in my pocket. "Allison, *you're the best!*"

A huge smile lit up her face before she headed for the lunch line.

Getting Even

That night I was too excited to sleep. So I got up and found my diary.

I am in a much better mood than when I last wrote. Allison, Mrs. Evans's new assistant, is going to speak with her about helping me prepare for the audition. I am so excited, but can I improve my technique enough to have a chance at the 'Stars and Stripes' solo? Everyone is better than me and prettier.

I put my diary back in its secret place, crawled into bed, closed my eyes and fell fast asleep.

"What are you doing up there? Are you crazy?" yelled Laura.

"I'm doing the snowball ballet!" I called back, dancing along the top of a snow pile.

Snowballs flew wildly around me, hitting my face, arms and legs.

"Come down. Stop dancing, Jo. *Stop dancing*!"

"No, I'll *never stop* dancing. NEVER."

"It's not pretty up there."

"Pretty, pretty! Who cares? I'm dancing."

I leapt off the snow pile like an injured bird, falling,

falling, twisting and falling. The ground moved closer and closer.

"Help!"

My heart pounded loudly when I opened my eyes. I realized with relief that it was early dawn and I was in my own bed. I knew I'd dreamt something important, which was swiftly slipping away. I couldn't bring it back.

In the dim light, I saw Allison's box by my bureau. I got up, opened it and took out her toe shoes. I tied the ribbons together and placed them over the corner of my mirror. Her toe shoes dangled against it as if they were dancing.

That day, on my way home from school, I thought about the audition. Leslie Louise would be there. No doubt she'd be picked. She was, after all, the better dancer. Even so, I wouldn't let her or Laura stop me! My technique would improve with Allison's help. That alone was enough.

At home, I gobbled down two of Mom's warm oatmeal raisin cookies before I picked up the phone and dialed Allison's number.

"Oh, hi!" exclaimed Allison. "I was just thinking about you. I have good news. Mrs. Evans will let us use the Grange after class every Saturday until the audition."

"*No way!*" I couldn't believe my luck.

"Yes, and we'll work on your jumps, turns and a few other steps."

"That's great."

"See you Saturday. Tell your mom that you'll be staying later and bring your permission slip."

"OK. Thanks, Allison, Bye."

After hanging up, my thoughts returned to Laura and how miserable she'd been to me. She wasn't getting away with being so nasty without some consequence. I began to form a plan on how to get even.

On Saturday, I was prepared for whispering and giggling when I entered the Grange. Everyone was preoc-
cupied so I did some stretches.

Mrs. Evans approached me smiling pleasantly. "Allison said you are auditioning for the 'Stars and Stripes'
solo and that you'll be practicing after class today.
Please have your mother call me right away about the
arrangements."

"I will," I said, handing her the crumbled permission slip. "Thanks for letting us use the Grange."

"My pleasure," replied Mrs. Evans. Then, addressing everyone, she said, "Class begins in five minutes."

I found an empty chair beside Laura, who was faced away from me, and sat down. This was the perfect opportunity to get even with her. When Mrs. Evans announced that class was starting, Laura bounded up and turned toward me. I stuck my foot out just in time to trip her. Immediately I pushed my dance bag where my foot had been. Laura landed with a deafening crash on her right knee, screamed, and fell in a heap, sobbing. *Yeah,* I thought, *my strategy worked!*

Everyone rushed to her. Mrs. Evans calmly sat down on the floor imploring Laura to stop crying and sit up. Once she was sitting, Mrs. Evans asked Laura to straighten her leg. As she did, I saw that her knee was bright red and badly scraped. I began to have regrets about what I'd done. Allison fled to the kitchen for ice while Mrs. Evans talked to Laura.

"You'll be fine but you must ice your knee fifteen minutes and then rest it several times today. It should feel better in a day or so. Alright, Ladies, do some stretches while I call Laura's mother."

Leslie Louise hovered over Laura as Allison rubbed an ice cube slowly over the red area.

Laura looked up at me. "You did this, *you witch!*"

Her words hit like a brick. Everyone stared at me. I insisted that Laura had tripped over my bag. She was denying it when Mrs. Evans interrupted.

"It was an accident," she stated. "Stop squabbling. Allison will teach while I help Laura leave. Mrs. Prebble, will you find us some music please?"

During the class, Leslie Louise glared at me as if she were shooting me poison darts. I couldn't concentrate on the barre work or the center floor combinations. Feeling strangely weak and sweaty, I told Mrs. Evans I wasn't feeling well and left.

I kept reliving Laura's fall and hearing her scream as I walked home. Laura could have really been hurt, even broken her leg. Unease gnawed at my mind like a rat gnawing wood. Maybe I should apologize. Maybe I shouldn't. Laura deserved it. My thoughts circled round and round.

Later that afternoon Allison called to see if I was OK. I'd totally forgotten about our practice time in all the turmoil. She said not to worry; we'd practice next week. She didn't ask about my part in Laura's fall. I was grateful.

The next day, after a restless night, I phoned Laura. Naturally, she didn't want to talk with me. "Wait!" I insisted. "Don't hang up. I told you I'd get even with you for hurting my feelings but I didn't want you to get so badly injured. I'm sorry."

A dead silence came from the other end. Then, the only sound was the click of the phone when Laura hung up. Tears slid down my cheeks as I thought about what I had done.

The following Saturday Laura returned to class. We ignored each other, barely making eye contact.

After class, Allison and I stayed later to practice jumps, leaps and arabesques.

She suggested that I deepen my plié to get more height while doing my jetés and she told me to pick a focal point in the room, to stare at, for better balance during arabesques. Allison pointed out that my knees weren't straight during my leaps, which I hadn't realized. I learned so much that afternoon. I knew I'd made the right decision to work with Allison.

❧

As the weeks went on, I felt a bit more self-confident. I even forgot about my drooping eyelid. I continued to keep my distance from Leslie Louise and Laura by ignoring them during Saturday classes.

With the audition rapidly approaching, I feared I would freeze up and forget what I'd learned. Mostly, I worried that my drooping eyelid would affect my chances. I phoned Allison.

"I'm feeling really nervous about the audition. Everyone else looks so good," I stated, skirting the real issue. "And what if I forget the combinations?"

"You're just having last-minute jitters. That's normal. After all, this is your first audition. Next time, you'll know what to expect. So forget about what might happen and don't worry about the outcome."

"That makes good sense."

"Oh, I almost forgot to tell you that Mrs. Evans will be driving me to the audition, so I'll be there rooting for you."

"*Oh, fabulous*, that's the best news! Thanks for everything, Allison. You're a true friend. See you at the Old Opera House."

I hung up the phone, went to my room and sat before the mirror staring at my face. Gently lifting my left eyelid, I thought I'd like the change. I didn't, which was just as well; my eyelids would never be even. Then, for some weird reason, I wondered why a pretty face was so important. I'd always thought it was, but maybe it wasn't. Maybe there was more to me than the way I looked.

The Audition

A few days later, Mom drove me to Boston where she left me off outside the Old Opera House. I entered its lobby, a large elegant room with a high ceiling, pink marble floor, and huge crystal chandeliers. Noisy, long-legged girls in tights and leotards were everywhere. *This is so exciting...a real theater!* I thought, pushing my way through the crowd.

As I passed the theater doors, I saw the stage. It had gold carvings bordering it and a deep-blue velvet curtain drawn back to expose several portable barres and a piano. What a difference from the shabby Exeter High School stage!

I spotted Allison and Mrs. Evans, who would drive us home, in the far corner of the lobby. Leslie Louise, Laura and several of Mrs. Evans's dancers were already there. Not long after I joined them, a heavy-set, short man in a neat, grey suit entered the lobby, shut the theater doors and introduced himself as Mr. Wilson. He instructed the teachers to line up their students. Then, he handed each girl a number to pin on her leotard. My number was seventy-seven, not my favorite but I hoped it would be lucky. Next, Mr. Wilson escorted the first fifteen girls to the stage. I could hear the piano and the teacher's distant voice.

Mr. Wilson returned a half an hour later for the next fifteen girls. This continued for a very long time. Finally, it was our turn.

"Go for it!" whispered Allison, as I left the lobby.

From the stage, I looked out on a sea of empty chairs, except for the front row where three judges sat. I recognized Mrs. Ashford and Miss Lawton from the *Alice in Wonderland* performance. The third judge was Mr. Mitchell, a handsome Negro and principal dancer from the New York City Ballet whom Mrs. Evans had mentioned. He performed occasionally as a guest dancer with the Boston Ballet. I couldn't believe that he was here for the audition!

A few minutes later, Madame Petrova, a tiny woman with slightly greying black hair and sparkling brown eyes, directed us to the portable barres. I'd heard that she'd defected from the Bolshoi Ballet several years ago.

"Welcome, Ballerinas, my name ees Madame Petrova," she said, in a heavy Russian accent. "Now, begin. Two demi-pliés, one grand plié. Move arm like thees. Make beautiful. Good, good. Go to tendus. Bring to feefth position, plié and relévé. Stay up. Very good. Feenish."

During the center floor work, Madame demonstrated a pirouette combination. Once we had practiced it, she had Leslie Louise and two other girls do it. I watched enviously as Leslie Louise effortlessly performed a perfect double turn ending right with the music.

Then Madame Petrova demonstrated a jeté combination. Instead of having everyone practice it, she turned to me and the girl behind me. "Number seventy-seven and number twenty pleeze to show combination."

I stared at her blankly. Maybe she had made a mistake. I looked around.

"Yes, number seventy-seven, ees you. Find place."

Suddenly my stomach felt queasy, my legs weak. As I walked to my place, I remembered Allison's advice to use my plié, spring up, point my toes and smile.

When the music began, a surge of energy lifted me up and down easily. It felt wonderful as everything blurred except the music and my movements. When the music stopped, I found I had landed. I looked anxiously toward Madame and the judges. She was busy conferring with the judges. My hopes faded.

"Numbers sixty-five and thirty-three pleese to do same," requested Madame Petrova.

After they danced, everyone moved diagonally across the stage doing grand jetés. The lively music was captivating and, forgetting my faded hopes, I danced. Finally, it was révérance. As we returned to the lobby, I felt an odd mixture of exhaustion and elation.

"You were wonderful, Jo," Allison exclaimed. "Mrs. Evans and I watched from the balcony. I think you've got a good chance."

"*You do?*"

"Yes, your grand jetés were super."

"Thanks to you," I said, smiling at her.

Just then, Mrs. Evans rushed down the stairs and gathered us together. "You girls looked so professional!

I'm proud of everyone. Now we'll just have to wait for the last group of dancers before we know the outcome."

While we were waiting, I overheard Laura speaking to Leslie Louise. "You're going to be picked. I just know it!"

"Well, if I am, my mother says she'll pay Viktor Lavrovsky to coach me. He's the famous Russian dancer who danced with the Bolshoi Ballet and defected along with Madame Petrova."

"Are you serious? That's fabulous."

"You bet. Mother will pay anything for me to have *the best*."

I'm sure she will, I thought enviously.

At last, Mr. Wilson appeared and everyone waited quietly as he announced that the judges had made their decisions.

"Will the girls with these numbers please go see Madame Petrova: numbers nine, twelve, thirty-six, seventy-five and seventy-seven."

Number seventy-five, that's Leslie Louise, *of course*. Number seventy-seven. ME, it couldn't be! Did he *really say number seventy-seven?*

I looked at Allison. "You made it!" she yelled, grabbing my shoulders and jumping up and down. I glanced over at Mrs. Evans. She was smiling broadly.

"Congratulations, girls," she said, hugging both Leslie Louise and me tightly. "Now hurry. Madame is waiting in the theater."

I felt proud as I moved through the crowd. What a feeling! Total strangers were congratulating *me*. As I approached Madame, a delightful energy flowed through me, warming my body and setting my face aglow. Although I would have to compete with Leslie Louise again, that didn't matter now.

Madame Petrova smiled as we joined the other finalists. She handed us a sheet of information. "Congratulations, Ballerinas, make to second audition. Now all five weel do same dance een April. Then, soloist ees chosen. Ees hard dance but I weel teach eet next week. Good luck. Meet next Saturday at studio two."

I rushed to Allison and took her hands. We jumped about, spun around and ended our celebration dance with a big hug.

As we drove home, I kept imagining the shock on my parents' faces when I told them I'd been picked as one of the finalists. I wondered why Mrs. Evans wasn't driving faster, if only she would!

❧

The following week, Mrs. Evans drove me to the Boston Ballet School where we met the other finalists to learn the "Stars and Stripes" routine. Laura had come with Leslie Louise to watch. She said hello to Mrs. Evans but looked right past me.

Laura followed Leslie Louise around like she was her shadow, but I didn't care. I didn't want a friend who ignored me *and* made fun of me.

Madame Petrova entered the studio a few minutes later, carrying five American flags. She placed them at

62

the back of the room and approached the group. There was a tall, blond girl named Jennifer, a small, bouncy girl named Susan with braces and a friendly smile, and a shy girl named Danielle, who kept twisting the strap of her dance bag. Leslie Louise stood by with her nose in the air.

"OK, Ballerinas, weel learn dance," said Madame. "Ees very hard dance. Weel do slowly. Begin here. Eight piqué turns, four relevé arabesques, tweest and salute."

Once we had tried it and repeated the difficult sections, she taught us the finale.

"Now do four single pirouette turns een place. Feefth turn ees double. Step to right and leap around en beeg circle to pick up flag. Grand battement holding flag like thees, another turn and feenish on knee, flag up."

Oh, no, I've never done a double turn. I hope this won't be as embarrassing as learning the waltz step in *Alice in Wonderland*. Thank goodness Madame Petrova is teaching this dance. I doubt she gets as easily upset as Miss Lawton.

"OK. Try up to tempo," announced Madame, as she played the record again.

I can't do my turns this fast. They're awful. I'm dizzy. I have to stop. I staggered to the side of the room and sat down. The room was spinning. I felt nauseous. Meanwhile, Leslie Louise finished the double turn perfectly.

After the rehearsal, Madame Petrova took me aside. Her eyes sparkled magically as she looked into mine. "Don't worry. You weel get eet. Mrs. Evans, or her assistant, weel help."

"Thank you, Madame. I hope so."

I picked up my bag, left the studio and paused in the empty hall considering things. *Madame Petrova seems to believe in me. But what does she think about my birth defect? Is she pretending not to notice? Does she think I'm ugly? Maybe...she doesn't even care!*

I felt light as air moving effortlessly down the hall to the dressing room. When I arrived, Mrs. Evans was outside the dressing room talking with Mrs. Marren. A tall middle-aged gentleman with dark piercing eyes gracefully approached them. In the dressing room, I heard Leslie Louise telling Laura that Viktor Lavrovsky, the Russian dancer that she'd mentioned last week would be mentoring her.

"How exciting!" Laura exclaimed. "You'll be trained like a Bolshoi ballerina. You're *sure* to win the solo now."

"Well, I should. Mr. Lavrovsky is the best teacher in the world. Mother insisted on hiring him. She'll do *anything* for my ballet career." Leslie Louise pulled a sweater over her leotard as she explained, "Mr. Lavrovsky was scheduled to retire when he returned to Russia. So, he and Madame Petrova hid the day the Bolshoi Ballet flew back to the Soviet Union. Their story was all over the news. Mr. Lavrovsky told reporters that he wanted the creative freedom to choreograph his own dances, which he couldn't do with the Bolshoi. Now, he and Madame teach, choreograph and mentor ballet students. Neither of them can *ever* return to Russia."

The dressing room door flew open as Mrs. Marren and Mrs. Evans entered. Mrs. Marren turned her stern-looking face toward Leslie Louise while Mrs. Evans put on her coat. "Come along, Darling, Mr. Lavrovsky must look at you before he'll agree to mentor you. Laura, we won't be long. Would you wait here?"

"No problem," Laura said, dismissively.

Mrs. Evans turned to me, her car keys jingling in her hand. "Are you ready to go, Jo?"

"All set," I replied, overjoyed to be leaving.

On the way home, Mrs. Evans discussed my practice times. "Unfortunately, I have a commitment Saturday afternoons, Jo. So, Allison will help you after I teach her the dance. Mrs. Marren has reserved the Grange, after your class, for Leslie Louise. But you can use it, for free, when she's done."

"That's great! Thank you *so* much."

Mrs. Evans is wonderful, I thought, as we approached Durham. She was taking me to the auditions *and* paying for the Grange. Maybe she really thought I had talent. And...she and Madame Petrova didn't seem to care *at all* about my drooping eyelid.

Practicing

The next week, after our Saturday class, Allison and I sat on the benches in the Grange entryway. Through the inner door we heard Viktor Lavrovsky rehearsing with Leslie Louise. His harsh voice rose above the music.

"Straighten knee. Leeft leg higher. Ees sloppy. Push self. Work harder! Do again, make look easy."

I could imagine Mr. Lavrovsky's eyes glaring at Leslie Louise as Mrs. Marren watched. *Thank goodness I'm not Leslie Louise*, I thought, surprised to find myself feeling a little sorry for her.

Just then the front door opened and Laura entered. "Waiting to rehearse?" she asked, looking at Allison, who nodded. Then, turning to me, Laura said, "I hate to tell you this, but you haven't got a chance against Leslie Louise."

I scowled at her. "Is that so?"

"Absolutely. Sorry, Allison, but you just can't compare with Mr. Lavrovsky. He's world-famous!"

I felt myself bristle with anger. How could Laura insult my friend so badly?

Before either of us could respond, Laura opened the interior door and left to join Leslie Louise.

"What a jerk! I never realized how mean she could

be," exclaimed Allison.

"You can say that again. Laura was my best friend but she's completely different now. It's sad. Anyway, she doesn't think I'm pretty," I said, before I realized it.

"Oh, how come?"

I couldn't believe it. Didn't Allison see my drooping eyelid? I hesitated, then blurted out, "'cause of my eye."

"Is that why? It's not that noticeable, you know. What happened to it?"

"I was born with my eyelid closed. I had an operation, but it wasn't very successful. My eyelid can only open partway."

"Oh," she paused, "I can't see breaking off a friendship because of it."

"Well, Laura wants to be popular. She thinks I'll keep her from being with the 'in crowd.'"

"Then, that's *her* problem."

"Her problem?"

"Yes, she's too afraid of differences and of what other people think."

Allison's statement shocked me. Maybe it *wasn't my problem*. If Laura didn't like me because of my looks, maybe it was *her* problem. Maybe I didn't have to think of myself as ugly because of what she, or anyone else, thought. Maybe it was more about what I thought of myself. Finally, I said, "I never thought of it that way."

"Being different isn't easy. I know. But everybody's different in some way." Allison stared off into space, and then continued, "There aren't any Chinese in Durham. I'm the only one in the high school. It's lonely at times."

I didn't say anything. It hadn't occurred to me that Allison would feel lonely or different, like me. She was so beautiful and always cheerful. Why hadn't I noticed? I was about to ask her more when the door opened and Leslie Louise, Laura, and Mrs. Marren filed out without looking our way. Mr. Lavrovsky stopped briefly to give Allison the John Philip Sousa record.

We gathered our dance bags, went into the room, and did some stretches. First we practiced the dance without the music, then with it several times.

"Allison, I'll never get these pirouette turns. They are *so* lousy!"

"You can't expect to get them perfect right away. You've got to practice pirouettes over and over, but these tips will help. Your preparation for this turn is from <u>fourth</u> <u>position</u> of the feet. Make it neat and clean by keeping your hips and shoulders from twisting. Plié and spring up into a high, turned-out <u>passé</u> with your standing leg straight. Like this." Allison demonstrated the position. "Notice that my arms are rounded in front of me, forming a nice circular shape, with my fingertips almost touching."

I practiced springing up to passé until I could balance a little longer. Allison was pleased. "Now add the turn. Find a spot in the room at eye level, maybe a smudge on the wall or that poster over there. Stare at it as long as possible while your body starts to turn. At the *very last minute*, snap your head around to find the object you chose to spot on again."

I stared at the poster on the wall and practiced the pirouettes. Only four out of ten turns were decent, but it was a beginning.

After rehearsing the entire dance three more times, I said, "I'm beat."

"OK. Let's stop and go get some food. I'm famished."

"Great idea. Let's go to Young's."

Allison locked the Grange and we walked to Young's Restaurant. Warm, fragrant smells of coffee and grilled steak and cheese greeted us as we entered and found a table. A tall, blond waitress took our order. While we waited for our food, Allison told me about the West Coast Ballet Academy.

"I really loved it there," she said with a sigh. "It's hard being here. I miss my grandparents and friends. The kids here aren't as friendly. Besides, because I was on scholarship, I could take five ballet classes a week. Here, I only assist Mrs. Evans's two Saturday classes. I love her. But, to be honest, the classes aren't hard enough. I'm losing all my technique."

The waitress brought our sandwiches and two hot chocolates. I took a bite of my sandwich and thought a minute. I hadn't realized any of this about Allison. Although, when I considered it, I knew that it was true. Other kids said little to her or they ignored her. And I had no idea she was so frustrated about losing her ballet technique. How could I have been so oblivious? Finally, I said, "Isn't there any way you could take more classes? Maybe join Mrs. Evans's dancers in Portsmouth or at the Boston Ballet School?"

"I have no way to get to Portsmouth. Both my parents work in Su Lee's Restaurant in Exeter so they can't drive me. I'd have to take the bus to Boston and I'd be exhausted going there after school. Mom and Dad say I have to wait and try out for the summer program. Besides, I'd rather wait. Partnering classes, which I love, are offered in the summer."

"Really! You mean dancing with *boys*?"

"Exciting, huh?" She pushed a stray lock of hair out of her eyes.

"Oh, yes! Is there any chance you can get in?"

"If I do well in the auditions, I will get a scholarship."

"Oh, I hope you do."

"Me, too. If I don't get it, I can't go. The summer program is terribly expensive. It includes room and board."

"Wow! You mean you'd live in Boston?" I asked, as I took the last bite of my sandwich.

"Yes! Isn't that exciting? I can't wait to be back in a city among different kinds of people. There are lots of Chinese in Boston and the ballet studio isn't far from Chinatown. There might even be other Chinese students auditioning for the summer program."

"By the way," I said, "I have an odd question. Is it true that all Chinese people look alike?"

Allison said nothing. She stared down at her empty plate before looking up. Her eyes drilled into mine with an intensity I'd never seen. "Where'd you get that *stupid* idea?'

Oh, no, I thought. *What have I done?* I hesitated, and then replied, "I heard it from some kids at school."

"And, you thought it might be true? How could you?"

I started to apologize but she continued. "*No, not all Chinese look alike.* That's utterly ridiculous."

Allison's words cut into me like a knife. I thought she might storm out of the restaurant, but she waited for me to speak.

There was a long pause as I wondered what to say. Why had I opened my big mouth and asked that dumb question? Why hadn't I thought about it first? I felt like an idiot. Allison and I had never been mad with each other, but she obviously hated me now. I thought I'd lost her friendship and her help with the audition. Acid-tasting saliva flooded my mouth. I swallowed hard to stop it. "Please forgive me, Allison. I am *so sorry.*"

She didn't accept my apology. Instead, she explained that some people made general statements, or stereotypes, that often weren't true, especially about people who looked differently from them. Allison said she'd heard some Chinese stereotypes that were deeply insulting. She paused before taking a sip of her hot chocolate.

My eyes began to tear up. My voice shook. "You're my best friend, Allison. I didn't mean to hurt your feeling."

Her face softened. "I know. You just didn't understand. Now you do."

"So, are we still friends?" I held my breath.

"Sure we are. Let's pay the bill and go."

Outside the restaurant, the crisp air struck our faces with a force so strong that it stung our cheeks. The temperature had grown too cold to linger. Before we separated, Allison invited me to her apartment after our next practice time. She wanted to show me her gypsy doll costume and pictures from *The Fantastic Toyshop* ballet. I gratefully accepted, relieved that Allison really had forgiven me.

I was introspective on my way home. I had insulted Allison just like Laura had insulted me. I hadn't meant to insult Allison, but I'd nearly lost her friendship. What if she hadn't been so forgiving? I made a vow that, from now on, I would guard my words and think before speaking.

৽৵৽

The following Saturday, Allison continued to coach me on my turns. "Remember about picking something to look at and snapping your head around."

I tried it and did six good single pirouettes. However, the double pirouette kept plaguing me. Once in a while, my body was positioned correctly, and I only had to snap my head around twice to complete the turn. Done correctly, it felt so easy. I knew, however, that I had to work harder. The double pirouette would be difficult to perform during the pressure of the audition.

"I think I'm beginning to get it!" I exclaimed.

"Good. Do a few more. Then let's work on the leaps."

Allison demonstrated leaping in a circle. I tried it. But by the fifth leap I was gasping for air.

"Don't stop breathing! Breathe in on the leap and out as you land."

We practiced the leaps for a while longer, changed clothes and walked to Allison's apartment. There, we found chocolate chip cookies and orange juice. As we ate, I marveled at the beautiful oriental scrolls hanging on the walls, and the Buddha statues.

Then Allison showed me her photographs and her costume. Her blouse was white satin with long, puffy sleeves. Over this was a black <u>bodice</u> with gold ties. The skirt was a delicate material with a red and blue floral design. It was as beautiful as the Boston Ballet costumes.

"I had a *great* time!" I said as I was leaving. "Let's go to my house next week."

"Super! Thanks."

Jo's Dream

Several weeks later, Mrs. Evans came to watch me practice. "The dance is looking super, Jo! Your leaps are higher, your legs straighter. Now, you must work on your double turn and your facial expression. You can be the loveliest dancer in the world, but, if you aren't enjoying the dance, the audience won't either."

I flinched. What about my expression...my face? Again, I agonized...would my drooping eyelid affect the judges' decision?

That night I sat at my mirror. While brushing my hair I began to study my delicate lips and high cheekbones. I became quiet, not thinking, just staring. After a long silence, I heard a small voice inside my head.

"Remember to value yourself above anyone else. You are precious just the way you are," it said.

Startled, I looked about.

Where had that voice come from? I wondered. Was I going crazy, hearing things? I ran my fingers gently over my eyes. "You are precious just the way you are," I repeated to myself. Precious...me? My grandfather would have said that. My drooping eyelid never stopped him from loving me.

With this thought, I felt the delightful lightness I'd felt before infuse my body. It was as though I had risen from the chair, suspended above it. I stayed with this pleasant feeling for a while. Then, I glanced at Allison's toe shoes and remembered the audition. Instantly the feeling left me. I was back sitting in the chair.

∽∾

As the weeks progressed, my double turn improved. I was enjoying the dance, smiling more readily.

One day, with the final audition only a week away, Mr. Lavrovsky and Leslie Louise were practicing while Mrs. Marren observed. Allison and I were waiting for Leslie Louise to finish when we heard Mr. Lavrovsky speaking with her. He was right by the inner door.

"Spectacular today," he said. Then, speaking to Mrs. Marren, he went on, "Eef Leslie Louise dances like that at audition, solo ees possible."

"I'm going to win 'cause you're coaching me. Besides, Jo's no competition. She's only got Allison helping her," added Leslie Louise.

"Never be content. Ees dangerous. There weel always be better dancers een future. Must keep working hard," insisted Mr. Lavrovsky.

"I suppose," she sighed.

"Of course, he's absolutely right," her mother reiterated. "You've got to work even harder. Until the audition you'll practice each day for two hours. I've already arranged it with Mrs. Evans. I *won't* have you settling for second-best."

The door opened. Leslie Louise walked into the entryway where we waited. She swept past us and turned around abruptly, swinging her ponytail side to side. "Are you ready for the audition, Jo?" Without waiting for my answer, she continued, "You'll *never* be as ready as I am." Then, looking directly at Allison, she said, "Mr. Lavrovsky has tons more experience than you. Why are you wasting your time?" She turned away slamming the heavy outside door behind her.

After Mrs. Marren and Mr. Lavrovsky left, I said, "*I can't stand Lousy Leslie.* I'm really upset that she insulted you."

"Thanks."

"Don't you want to say something nasty about her?"

"Of course, but we haven't got time to *waste on her.* Come on. Let's get started."

During the session, I rehearsed the dance facing the back of the Grange. It was extremely disorienting. My turns were especially difficult. I was used to focusing on the poster at the front of the room. When I commented on this, Allison explained. "At the audition you won't have a poster to look at. The same is true when you're performing. You might focus on an exit sign or the doors at the back of the theater. Today, focus on something you can see in this direction that's at eye level."

Allison sounded like I could win the audition! My energy soared. I practiced as though I were performing in the theater. I rehearsed the entire piece, facing the back of the Grange. Once I'd practiced it several times, even the dreaded double turn was slightly better.

That night I had a dream. I was practicing my turns

when suddenly I was in front of someone's house knocking at the door. It opened and I stood there in shock. The girl who answered the door looked just like me.

"Hello, my name is Jo Price," the girl said.

"But, but...my name is Jo Price, too...Are you me?"

"Yes, I am. I'm so glad you came. I love you."

I began to cry. The girl at the door came close and hugged me.

At that moment, I awoke. The bedroom was totally dark. *What a strange dream,* I thought. I wondered what it meant. A cool breeze came from the window. I got up, closed it and returned to bed. A warm sensation surrounded me as I fell back to sleep.

"Number 3, Jo Price," announced a tall woman dressed in black, holding a clipboard.

The music began. I started to dance but something stopped me. I looked up. Leslie Louise towered above me.

"Get out of my way!" I screamed.

Leslie Louise just stood there, smiling her pretty smile. I dodged to her side, but Laura appeared.

"I knew you wouldn't win," she taunted me.

"Your time is up, Ms. Price," said the woman in black as the spotlight grew brighter and brighter.

I opened my eyes. Sunlight was falling on my face.

What a night! I thought. My dreams haunted me the whole day and into the evening.

The Final Audition

Mom drove me to the Boston Ballet School on the day of the final audition. At the office we met a small, grey-haired woman who sat behind a cluttered desk. She wore bright red lipstick and smoked a cigarette that dangled dangerously from her lips.

"What can I do for you, Dearie?" she asked.

"I'm here for the final 'Stars and Stripes' audition."

She took a puff of her cigarette, crushed it out, and then said, "What's your name?"

"Jo Price from Mrs. Evans's Ballet School."

She quickly shuffled through a stack of papers. "Sign your name here," she instructed, handing me a paper and pen. "Mothers wait in studio two until we're ready to start. Can you show your mother the way?"

"Certainly."

I returned the signed paper and led Mom down the hall. Partway there we saw Leslie Louise stretching her legs in a perfect side split. She wore green eye shadow, lipstick and rouge. Her red hair was pulled neatly into a bun. She lifted herself up a few inches and twisted into a perfect forward split. I could not get into a perfect split, as hard as I tried. My legs were always four to five inches from the floor. During classes, Mrs. Evans often reminded us that everyone's body is different and that some people are more flexible than others.

"Oh, hi, Jo. Ready for the audition?" Leslie Louise asked sweetly.

"Absolutely," I lied.

Before I could say more, she looked up at Mom, "I'm Leslie Louise Marren. You must be Mrs. Price. Nice to meet you."

"Nice to meet you, too."

We continued down the hall. When we were out of hearing range my mother spoke. "She seems very nice."

"Well, she's *not*...not nice at all. If you knew her, you'd hate her too."

Mom gave me an inquisitive look but asked no questions. "Oh...I see," she said.

I left her in studio two with the other mothers and walked past Leslie Louise without acknowledging her. From the other end of the hallway, I could hear Jennifer, another finalist, going over the counts of the dance. When I entered the dressing room, Susan and Danielle, two of the finalists, were chatting as they dressed. I was pulling up my leotard when Mrs. Evans appeared with Leslie Louise.

"Oh, there you are, Jo. Are you excited?" asked Mrs. Evans.

I pinned back my short hair and nodded.

"I have the audition order here," she informed us. Scanning the paper that she held, she continued. "Leslie Louise, you're second and, Jo, you're fourth. If you girls want to leave the audition, for any reason, please remember to come and go quietly. OK. Let's go. It's about time."

We followed Mrs. Evans into studio two. A few minutes later Madame Petrova appeared and announced that the audition would begin. Everyone followed her into studio one where we sat with our mothers at the back of the room. The judges, whom I recognized from the first audition, sat at a table in front of a marked-off section of the floor. This indicated an imaginary stage where we would dance. It did not face the mirror. I sent a silent thank you to Allison for her tips on turning without one. The stage area was surrounded by portable stage lights. A pianist sat at the right of the judges.

Jennifer was the first dancer called. My hands grew

sweaty, my stomach queasy as she walked forward. When the pianist began, I noticed that Jennifer looked uneasy. She was off the beat and late picking up the flag. I felt sorry for her, especially at the end, when she looked like she wanted to cry. At the same time, I felt happy. She had obviously lost the audition. I would have a better chance of winning it.

Leslie Louise was next. She walked forward holding her head high and smiled confidently as the music began. All her steps were precise and energetic. I watched her do the four single turns and the double turn elegantly. She performed the high leaps impressively and ended gracefully on her knee with the flag held high. Her presentation and ballet technique were flawless.

My heart sunk. *I've lost the solo, just like in my dream*, I thought. My performance can't compare but I *am not* letting Leslie Louise's performance kill mine. I will dance even better, try even harder.

The judges were gesturing and talking enthusiastically as Leslie Louise walked past me to her mother and Mrs. Evans. I could hear Mrs. Marren behind me.

"You were spectacular, Darling. Wasn't she brilliant, Mrs. Evans?! I'm sure she's won. Don't you think so?"

"She has a good chance but remember there are three girls left to dance. We'll have to wait and see."

My mother, who had also overheard, gave me an inquiring look. I gave her my most confident smile, as if to say, "I'm fine. I'll do my best."

Susan was next. She walked to her place, looking composed. During the dance, however, she wobbled on the single turns and could not perform the double. She left the stage area with her head down. I didn't have time to register any emotions because Mrs. Evans approached me. "You're next, Jo. Go up there and break a leg!"

"No thanks," I retorted with a slight smile.

When my name was called, I took my place. My heart was pounding loudly. I was relieved to find that the lights shown so brightly that I could barely see the judges. Then the music began and I started my piqué turns.

Step, look, spin. Step, look, spin, I told myself. Now do two more and into the relévé arabesques. A little wobbly on that last arabesque. Oh, well. Salute now. OK, single pirouettes. Not bad. Now the dreaded double turn. Oh, no. My balance is off. Leaps are next. Yes. Up and down, good. Get the flag and keep it high, OK! Go down to the pose and smile.

It was over. The room was uncomfortably silent except for the scratching of pens. I wasn't sure what to do. So, I put the flag back in its original place.

Back at my seat, Mom gave me a big hug.

Next Mrs. Evans came over and whispered, "You were terrific!"

"I was?"

"Oh, yes! That's the best dancing you've ever done."

"Really? What about my double turn?"

"You were slightly off balance. It was hardly noticeable."

"That's good but I doubt I've won."

"We'll know shortly."

I was in a daze while, Danielle, the fifth dancer, performed. However, I noticed that, although her technique was satisfactory, she never smiled. Following her performance, the judges huddled together, while Madame Petrova conferred with Mrs. Evans and the other teachers. I watched the clock slowly move...five minutes, ten minutes, and then fifteen minutes. Finally, Mrs. Ashton stood up. She asked the five of us to join her at the judges' table. As I predicted, she pronounced Leslie Louise the winner. Then she continued, "Miss Jo Price, we have chosen you to be her understudy. Congratulations."

Me...Leslie Louise's understudy? Shocked, I mumbled my thanks to the judges. I hadn't considered being the understudy. If Leslie Louise gets sick or injured, I would dance the solo. Otherwise, I wouldn't. And...she *never* got sick or injured. Suddenly I realized that my mind had wandered. I quickly turned my attention to Mrs. Ashton, who was addressing the three other dancers. "The Boston Ballet Company thanks you for your time. We hope you will attend our future auditions. You have earned free tickets to the performance. They will be ready at the box office the night of the show. Again, we thank you."

Madame turned to Leslie Louise and me as the others were leaving. "Performance ees May twentieth, at eight o'clock, een Old Opera House. Mrs. Evans weel know schedule for rehearsals soon. Jo, you do same rehearsals. Good job, dancers," she said. Her eyes sparkled as she shook our hands.

When I returned to Mom, she hugged me saying, "I'm so proud of you."

"But," I protested, "I didn't get the solo."

"What's it matter? You did a great job."

Before I could speak, Mrs. Evans added, "You certainly did." She had just finished congratulating Leslie Louise. "Now aren't you glad you auditioned? Being the understudy is a *huge* honor."

I didn't know what to say. I'd been honored; however, I didn't feel overjoyed. Being Leslie Louise's understudy meant *enduring her again*. Why was I feeling sorry for myself? After all, I was runner up. Wasn't understudy good enough? My feelings were all mixed up.

When I didn't respond, Mrs. Evans gave me a quick hug and went off to talk with Madame Petrova.

Just then, Leslie Louise walked past me and turned around. "So sorry, Jo. Remember...I told you I would win. Naturally, Allison's teaching skills could never compare to those of Mr. Lavrovsky. We're calling him tonight. He'll help me refine the solo."

After she left, I faced my mother and said, "What'd I tell you? She's *disgusting*."

"Forget her, Jo. Leslie Louise is just a spoiled brat." Then, looking at her watch, she stated, "Your dad should be home. Let's go tell him your news. It's time to celebrate."

The Reactions

Dad sat on the sofa reading the newspaper when we returned. He put it down and asked about the audition. I told him I'd been chosen to understudy the soloist. Immediately he jumped up, grabbed my waist and twirled me around.

"Wahoo!" he shouted. He stared at me after we stopped spinning. "You don't seem terribly excited, Jo."

"I'm excited but, Leslie Louise, who won the solo, is so mean to me. Besides, she's never sick. So I won't perform."

"Is it really that bad?"

"Yes, Dad, *it's bad*."

"Ignore her," demanded Mom, repeating the same unrealistic solution she'd suggested earlier.

"Mom, you don't understand. It's impossible ignoring Leslie Louise, *truly impossible*."

Dad interrupted. "Let's forget about her and celebrate with your mom's world-famous spaghetti."

As Mom headed to the kitchen, I left for my room, tossed my dance bag aside and flopped onto my bed. Mom thought it was easy tolerating Leslie Louise and Dad didn't know her. I couldn't discuss Leslie Louise with them anymore.

After dinner I excused myself, and rushed into the

study to call Allison.

"Hi, Jo," she said. "I expected to hear from you sooner. What happened? How'd you do?"

"Well, I'm Leslie Louise's understudy. Great, huh?"

"Fabulous, Jo. I'm thrilled for you."

"Don't get me wrong. I'm really excited being the understudy. At the same time, I'm really upset. Leslie Louise is sure to perform." I sighed deeply.

"Yes, she will. So what?"

I couldn't believe Allison's words. *So what?*

"Ya, so what?" she repeated. "I've asked you this before and I'll ask it again. You love to dance, don't you?"

"Of course I do."

"Well then, what's it matter? There'll be plenty of other dancing challenges."

I considered this a minute, then said, "You're right, Allison. I guess this isn't my last chance, is it?"

"Hardly! So, when do you rehearse?"

"I don't know. Mrs. Evans might have the schedule by Saturday. Hey, want to go to Young's for ice cream to celebrate after our class? It's on me."

"Great. I'd love that."

After hanging up, I thought about our conversation. Something Allison said made me recall my mother's words, *Leslie Louise is just a spoiled brat.* Then it hit me. I'd been acting like a spoiled brat, too. Allison was right. I didn't need to be the soloist or even the understudy. I loved dancing. That was all that mattered, and, strangely, my drooping eyelid hadn't bothered me. I knew it hadn't influenced the judges' decision 'cause, to be honest about it, Leslie Louise really was the better dancer.

❦

The next Saturday, I arrived at the Grange early. Leslie Louise and Laura were already in the entryway waiting for class. Pleasant music from the earlier class came through the closed door. I was debating about congratulating Leslie Louise when she turned to Laura and said, "Let me introduce you to my new understudy, Miss Jo Price. She gets to stand behind me and copy everything I do."

Instantly they broke into hysterical laughter.

"I'm not copying any of your mistakes," I replied, happy at my quick response.

"I NEVER make mistakes!" she giggled.

Suddenly the entryway was crowded with dancers hugging and congratulating Leslie Louise. Thankfully the younger students were leaving. So I left to prepare for my class.

I didn't care if they ignored me. I was proud of myself whether anyone besides Allison acknowledged me or not. Then, to my surprise, Stacey, the girl who'd retrieved my shoe during the *Alice in Wonderland* performance, congratulated me as soon as I entered the room. "Thanks a lot, Stacey, but I couldn't have done it without help." I nodded toward Allison, who, upon overhearing me, rushed over to give me a warm hug.

"*Gracias, Amiga!*" Allison replied.

Speaking softly, Stacey inquired, "Sometime, Allison,

would you help me with my turns? I'm having a terrible time with them."

"Sure. I'll give you my phone number after class," she answered, as we took our places.

During the class, I thought about Stacey. Although I hardly knew her, she'd always been nice to me. She didn't have many friends here or at school. I wondered if she'd had some difficult times similar to mine.

After class, Mrs. Evans spoke to Leslie Louise and me about the schedule. "Your first rehearsal and costume fitting is this Friday afternoon at three-thirty at the Boston Ballet School. Dress rehearsal is the following Thursday at the Old Opera House and the performance is there on Friday." Then, turning to me, she said, "Jo, you have to be at all rehearsals and, assuming Leslie Louise performs, you get to see the performance for free."

After Allison gave Stacey her phone number, we went outside where we watched Leslie Louise and Laura, chatting and giggling, get into Mrs. Marren's car.

I'm so glad I have a new best friend, I thought as they drove away.

Putting my arm around Allison's shoulder, I said, "Let's go to Young's for that ice cream I promised you." Then I shouted to Stacey, who'd gone ahead of us, "Come back and join us for ice cream. I'm treating. It's time to celebrate!"

Stacey abruptly twirled around. Smiling broadly, she joined us.

The Costume Fitting

When Friday finally came, Mom picked me up at school and we headed to Boston. In the car, I began twisting and untwisting the straps of my dance bag.

"You're awfully quiet, Jo. What's wrong?"

"I'm worried about the class we'll take before our rehearsal."

"What about it?"

"The members of the company will be there. I've never taken an adult class. It's a bit intimidating."

"Sounds exciting."

"For sure, but the center floor combinations will be complicated. I won't know all the steps."

"You'll do fine, Sweetheart," Mom stated with finality.

She didn't understand my anxiety. So I didn't pursue the conversation. I took a deep breath to calm myself down. Why was I getting so worked up? No one would judge me. After all, I wasn't a professional ballet dancer. I wouldn't learn advanced steps for many years.

We drove in silence to the Boston Ballet School. Mom left me at the door, where she would return for me later. I went up the stairs, changed and headed to studio one. The door was closed but I heard Miss Lawton's penetrating voice announcing the start of class.

Inside, the room was packed with twenty or more professional dancers and students. I found a place behind Leslie Louise, who was already at the barre. The plié music began and Miss Lawton demonstrated. Surprisingly, I followed every warm-up exercise fairly well. After the barre work, Madame Petrova entered, carrying two flags and a record. She ushered us, along with Mrs. Marren, out of the class. As we walked down the hall, I realized that I'd been worrying about the center floor work for nothing. We weren't even staying for it.

In studio two, Madame Petrova said, "Hello, girls. Are your muscles warm eenough to start? Good." Then, to Mrs. Marren, she said, "You can seet at the back of the room eef you vant to vatch."

Once Mrs. Marren was seated, I positioned myself behind Leslie Louise. Madame began. "Leeft your arms a leetle more here," she advised. "Ees good, girls. Now move more sharply on the passés. More eexpression. Good, good."

After rehearsing the dance for an hour, Leslie Louise and I headed to the costume room. On the way, we didn't speak with each other.

In the costume room, a very large woman with a round face and unkempt blond hair sat at a sewing machine sewing a long lavender skirt. With effort she detached herself from her chair and picked up two large circular boxes.

"Are you girls here for the 'Stars and Stripes' costumes?"

We nodded.

"Which one of you is the soloist?"

"I am," replied Leslie Louise.

"Good. Come here. Let's see," said the seamstress as she opened one of the boxes. "Try this on." She handed Leslie Louise a red-and-white striped tutu attached to a sleeveless blue leotard with gold epaulettes. Leslie Louise slipped into the costume easily. "Perfect fit. Super. Here's the hat." The seamstress pulled a small, blue pillbox hat with red strips from the box and handed it to her. "OK, take your costume off and bring it home."

To me, she said, "Try this costume." I pulled it on over my leotard and tights.

"Good heavens, it's huge! Wait a minute. I'll remedy that." She began pinning in the costume at the back. "Bend forward. How does it feel?"

"Fine, just right." I looked down at the tutu. It was short, sticking out no more than eight inches. The top layer was a shiny, red-and-white striped satin. Under that were four or five layers of white netting. Whenever I moved, the tutu bounced about, encouraging me to dance. I took it off reluctantly.

While she sewed, I explored the room. The playing cards we had worn stood in one corner. Beside me was an open trunk filled with different-colored leotards and a pile of gray-green toe shoes that smelled rancid from being dyed. At the other side of the room, there hung a white dress with an embroidered, pearl bodice. A diamond tiara rested over it, reminding me of the snowflake costumes from *The Nutcracker*.

"All done," stated the seamstress, handing me the costume box.

I thanked her and walked past the office into the dressing room. To my surprise, Leslie Louise waited there. Seeing my puzzled look, she said, "My mother is *still* talking with Madame. I thought we'd be home by now."

"Oh." I hung my costume on a hook and began changing into my street clothes. We were alone. The silence felt heavy. Finally, she spoke.

"You know something?"

"What?" I asked, not sure I wanted to know.

"My mother is such a *pain*. She is *always* around."

"Oh, really?" I asked, as if I hadn't noticed.

"Yes. I can't wait to turn fourteen next year. Then, I'll attend Millbrook Ballet Academy. It's a four-year boarding school and I'll be away from her."

I stared at Leslie Louise, unable to respond. Was she really confiding in me? She had seemed to like having her mother around but, evidently, she didn't. I couldn't blame her. I wouldn't want Mom hovering over me constantly. At last I said, "I see."

It was uncomfortably quiet until Mrs. Marren entered some minutes later. As Leslie Louise walked toward the door, I said, "See you tomorrow."

"OK. See you then."

While Mom and I rode home, I thought things over. What was life like for Leslie Louise? Did her mother dictate her every move? Did her father live with them? Though Leslie Louise had been mean, I felt oddly concerned. I even felt a smidgen sorry for her.

"You're quiet tonight, Jo. Are things OK?"

"Yeah, everything's fine. Mom..." How could I tell her I was glad she wasn't a <u>ballet</u> <u>mother</u> like Mrs. Marren?

"What?" Mom asked.

I took a breath, and then simply stated, "I love you."

"I love you, too, Honey," she replied.

Dress Rehearsal

The afternoon of dress rehearsal, Allison watched me practice the solo in my costume. We had pushed the living room furniture out of the way to make an imaginary stage. Allison put on the "Stars and Stripes" record that she'd brought and I danced for her.

"You're looking spectacular," she said.

"Do you really think so?"

"Absolutely! You're right on the music and your expression is good." She glanced at her watch. "I'd better get going. Will you be in school tomorrow?"

"Yes, but not until lunchtime, Mom is letting me sleep late."

"Great. See you then. I can't wait to hear about dress rehearsal."

After she left, I went to my room, took off my costume and packed my dance bag. A little later, Mom came in carrying a present.

"For me?" I was shocked. What could she have?

"None other!" she exclaimed.

I unwrapped her gift, and then gasped. She'd bought me a small cosmetic bag containing lipstick, rouge, eye makeup and a mirror.

"I don't believe it!" I exclaimed, as I jumped up and wrapped my arms around Mom's neck. "Thank you, thank you!"

"Remember, this is performance makeup only," she insisted. "But...I guess, since you're thirteen now, you can use the lipstick sometimes!" Mom gave me a smile, then left.

"You're great!" I called after her.

As I rubbed on the rouge, I recalled how Laura had applied her mother's make up on me the year before. *Wow, things have changed!* I thought. *Now Mom says I can wear lipstick, at least sometimes, and Laura isn't my best friend.* I stared at the eye makeup. Would it make my drooping eyelid more noticeable? Did I care? No. Laura still didn't think I was pretty. Did I care? No.

I carefully applied the blue eye shadow and smiled at my reflection in the mirror.

"You look lovely, Sweetheart," Mom remarked as I gathered my costume and dance bag. "Now we'd better go. It's time this understudy was on the road!"

At the Old Opera House, she left me off and went to park the car. Mom planned to wait for me in the theater after the "Stars and Stripes" solo. I left her feeling very professional, walking in the backstage door alone.

Inside, I passed a dressing room where several dancers peered into a long mirror, applying makeup. Through the walls, I heard the instruments in the orchestra pit preparing. After changing into my costume, I joined some dancers limbering up in the hall. I'd begun my pliés when I realized that I hadn't seen Leslie Louise. Where was she? Maybe she was late. She was never sick.

A few minutes later, the stage manager gave the five-minute curtain call. Everyone rushed around, making last-minute adjustments to their hair, costume or shoes. I looked out into the dimly-lit theater for Leslie Louise. She wasn't there. So I took my place in the wings, where I saw Mrs. Ashford, Miss. Lawton and Madame Petrova standing on the stage with a group of ballerinas. Mrs. Ashford turned and gestured to the lighting director at the back of the theater. I knew it would be a long night coordinating all the lighting and music cues. "Give us a bit more blue light at center stage, Ben," yelled Mrs. Ashford. "A bit more still. Good, just right."

I watched as the lighting changes caused the dancers' lavender dresses to become a deep blue-violet. The stage seemed transformed.

"OK, let's begin. Places, please," demanded Mrs. Ashford. "Close the curtains."

My heart began to pound as I heard the swish of the moving curtains. My palms started sweating, my stomach churning. *Where was* Leslie Louise? Why wasn't she here?

The orchestra played a few measures of the introduction as the curtain opened. The ballerinas performed their beautiful waltz piece flawlessly and gracefully left the stage. A delightful <u>duet</u> was next. The solo would follow. I could hardly watch the duet. I'd grown so anxious. *I'll have to do the solo if Leslie Louise doesn't show up in two more minutes*, I thought, nervously rubbing my palms together. I could do it. If I had to, I could do it.

The dance ended, the couple left the stage and the lights dimmed. Trembling, I took the flag, laid it at the back of the stage where it was to be picked up, and took my place. The music started. The lights came on. I began to dance.

"Stop, stop," screamed Mrs. Ashford to the conductor. Then she asked me, "Where's the soloist?"

"She isn't here," I replied.

"Not here? Where is she?" Her brow furrowed; she looked severely annoyed.

"I don't know."

"Well, that's great!" Mrs. Ashford stated sarcastically. "OK, time's wasting. Start again."

I took my place and the music began. I started twirling, faster and freer, like in a dream. Tingling with energy, I stepped into the arabesque right as the cymbals crashed. Then, to the brilliant notes of the piccolo, I twisted and saluted. Suddenly, I was leaping, soaring higher and higher as the music grew in intensity to its crescendo. After spinning easily on the double turn, I twirled to the flag, picked it up and slid onto my knee.

It was over. The applause echoed around the theater. The professional dancers continued to clap for me! I was stunned but remembered to curtsy before leaving the stage. As I rushed into the wings, Madame Petrova approached me.

"Jo, you, a wonderful, wonderful dancer! Someday make a ballerina!" She paused, as if figuring something out, and then said, "Nobody has heard from Leslie

Louise. So must be prepared to dance solo tomorrow eef she's not here."

"She'll be here." I reassured Madame Petrova while really hoping Leslie Louise wouldn't show up. "I doubt anything will keep her away, especially since she's missed tonight's rehearsal."

"We can't be sure. Life ees strange. Maybe you weel dance."

I thanked her, returned to the dressing room, changed, and then met my mother in the theater.

"Oh, Jo, you danced *so* well. Too bad your dad wasn't here," she said, hugging me tight. "Hey, what happened to Leslie Louise? Is she sick?"

"Nobody knows. If she's not here tomorrow, I get to dance the solo again!"

"That'd be terrific! We'll have to wait and see."

I wanted to call Allison, but it was midnight when we got home. The next day, I met her in the school cafeteria and told her every detail of the dress rehearsal. She was ecstatic when I told her that I might dance the solo for the performance.

The Performance

After school I went to Jensen's Gift Shop to buy a necklace with a toe shoe charm for Allison. The saleswoman put it in a box and wrapped it in pretty pink paper. I couldn't wait to give it to Allison.

At home, I put her gift in my dance bag, donned my favorite party dress and my shiny black shoes. I took my costume and bag into the kitchen where my parents were waiting.

As we drove to the theater, I tried to calm myself. We hadn't heard from Leslie Louise or Mrs. Evans. So I would, most likely, dance. I kept reminding myself that I could do it again. To be safe, I kept reviewing the dance in my mind. Step, turn, step.

My parents left me off at the backstage door. "Good luck, Princess. I hope you get to dance," Dad said.

"Me, too."

"We'll save you a seat just in case Leslie Louise is here," added Mom.

I bounced through the door, my dance bag trailing behind me. Backstage company members were busy putting on makeup, tying toe shoes or getting into costume. I searched the dressing rooms without finding Leslie Louise. Madame Petrova, Miss Lawton and Mrs. Ashford were nowhere in sight.

I couldn't believe my luck. Tonight Mom, Dad, Allison and Mrs. Evans would be in the audience! I dashed into a dressing room, changed, applied my makeup and started stretching when Leslie Louise appeared wearing *her costume*. Instantly I felt like I'd been punched in the stomach. My excitement vanished. I stared down at my costume, wanting to tear it off. How foolish I'd been to assume I would dance.

Leslie Louise approached me with a scowl. "Why are *you* dressed to perform?"

I stumbled over my words, embarrassed. "Well I...didn't. I thought... you weren't here."

"Didn't Miss Lawton tell you? I called her this morning."

"No, she must have been too busy."

"Didn't you think to check the stage when you arrived? Miss Lawton had me <u>mark</u> the dance to get used to the stage. Obviously I couldn't do that yesterday."

I hated the way she spoke to me, like I was an idiot. I chose to ignore her comment and changed the subject instead. "So, why weren't you at dress rehearsal?"

"On our way here, our car began making a horrible grinding noise. Mom pulled over before the car stopped completely. Then we walked about a mile to the nearest house to call for a tow truck. We waited hours. It was a nightmare. No one was answering the box office phone when we got home."

"Sorry to hear that," I managed to say, though I really wasn't sorry. "I should change out of this costume."

"Yes, you should." Then, before I was out the door,

Leslie Louise called after me, "Oh, Jo...enjoy the show!"

"Thanks. You're *so kind!*" I couldn't hide my sarcasm. The old nasty Leslie Louise was back, *no more confiding in me, that's for sure,* I thought.

I rushed into the dressing room, snatched my things and pushed my way through the crowd into the bathroom. I slammed the door shut, burst into tears and blew my nose. Thrusting the tissue into the trash, I yanked off the costume. I forced myself to take some deep breaths. Calmer, I put on my party dress and carried my things to the stage door where I gave Madame Petrova the costume.

"There ees reception after show, Jo. You come, yes?"

"Sure," I said, trying to sound upbeat.

I found Allison sitting with my parents in the audience. Mrs. Marren and Laura were seated a few rows closer to the stage.

"Leslie Louise is here, huh?" Dad remarked.

"Yup," I managed to say, forcing myself not to cry.

He put his arm around my shoulders. "Too bad, Princess, I wanted to see you perform, but there'll be plenty more performances."

"That's right, Honey," agreed Mom.

A lump formed in my throat. I nodded.

Later, after composing myself, I handed Allison her gift.

"What's this?"

"It's just a little thank-you gift."

"You shouldn't have!"

"Go on, go on. Open it!"

Allison ripped off the wrapping paper, opened the box and exclaimed, "Oh, Jo, it's gorgeous! I've always wanted a necklace like this. Thank you *so* much." She placed it around her neck, then asked, "How's it look?"

"Great, really great!"

In a few minutes, Mrs. Evans joined us and the lights dimmed. The curtain opened on the ballerinas dressed in lavender. I marveled at how different their dance looked from the audience.

After the duet, the curtain opened on Leslie Louise as she began to twirl effortlessly. She twisted and saluted with military precision, eyes sparkling, face glowing. Her leaps were high and strong, the double turn flawless. She ended elegantly on her knee with the flag held high. The audience went wild. I even found myself clapping.

Allison leaned over. "Prima ballerina wasn't too bad, was she?"

"No," I had to admit.

At intermission, Mrs. Evans insisted that we come to the reception following the performance. Then she went to help put out the food.

The rest of the performance was awe-inspiring, especially the solo by Mr. Mitchell who had been one of the judges. He appeared to be suspended in air during his dynamic leaps across the stage. His perfectly executed turns brought gasps from the audience. Everyone instantly rose to their feet after his dance. Yells of <u>bravo</u> rang throughout the theater as he bowed and left the stage. The applause continued, so Mr. Mitchell returned to the stage for another bow followed by Mrs. Ashford, who presented him with a laurel wreath that he took, bowing to her and, one last time, to the audience.

After the performance, my parents, Allison, and I joined the reception in the lobby. It was filled with people talking and laughing. Some dancers still wore their costumes. Mrs. Evans ladled out punch at a table full of food. Nearby stood a podium beside which hung a banner that read Patrons and Friends of Boston Ballet.

As we ate cookies and drank punch, more dancers from the performance arrived including Leslie Louise, who had already found Laura. I also spotted Stacey with her parents in the crowd. Allison and I were headed to her when Mrs. Ashford went to the podium and signaled for quiet. Everyone stopped talking and turned to her. She had two large envelopes in her hand.

"Every year it gives me great pleasure to announce the Patrons and Friends of the Boston Ballet's Scholarships to Briar Point Ballet Camp. These scholarships are awarded to two girls, between the ages of ten and fourteen, who have shown the most progress during the past year. This year's July scholarship goes to Miss Brenda Vaughn and the August scholarship goes to Miss Jo Price."

There was a roar of applause. Stunned, my heart pounding, I looked around.

Did she say *my* name...for ballet camp? People were looking at me. I moved, as if I were in a dream, to the

podium where Mrs. Ashford shook my hand and gave me one of the envelopes. I thanked her and returned to my parents.

Dad greeted me with his broad grin, "Princess, what a surprise!"

Mom gave me a kiss on the cheek and said, "You've faced many challenges and overcome them, Sweetheart!" I knew Mom really meant it. Her face was flushed, her smile huge.

Allison, Stacey and some girls from my class crowded around, congratulating me. Even Laura and Leslie Louise came over. They acted polite but curt. I didn't care.

Mrs. Evans hugged me, and then said, "Jo, you've worked hard. You deserve this! I hope you'll enjoy camp."

"Thanks, Mrs. Evans. I will. I know I will!"

My parents and I were about to leave the theater when Madame Petrova approached us. "Jo, thees ees special award. Special, like you."

"Thank you, Madame," I said, closing the theater door behind me.

At home, I sat before my mirror, gently wiping the makeup off my eyelids, smiling at myself. My drooping eyelid seemed to smile back at me. Both eyes sparkled as I reviewed the events of the past two days: Mom's gift, dancing the solo at dress rehearsal, my friends congratulating me and the scholarship. I'd never felt so happy, so grateful.

Me...at ballet camp! UNBELIEVABLE. I couldn't

wait. Attending Briar Point Ballet Camp was *far better* than dancing the solo! I marveled at the possibly that someday I might really become a ballerina!

Part Two

Arriving at Camp

My heart raced as we turned off the Maine Turnpike toward Briar Point Ballet Camp. Storm clouds hung above the deep blue ocean; its white surf pounded the rocky shore. A chill spread through me. In last night's dream, I was swimming alone in the ocean, no land in sight. Frightened, I awoke with my sheets twisted around me like a tightly coiled cobra squeezing its prey. Now, to my relief, our car turned away from the shoreline into the forest.

"Where do we turn next?" asked Dad, from the front seat of the car.

"Take the first road after the village of Briar Cove toward Briar Point," answered Mom. She was studying a map to the camp. "It should be Wilton Drive."

"Keep your eyes open, Jo."

"OK, Dad," I replied.

Raindrops began to fall. This wasn't the sunny, easygoing day I'd imagined. It was rainy, gray and cold. I felt apprehensive. The dream continued to haunt me. Was it a negative omen about camp?

To change my mood, I thought about my friend, Allison, who was already halfway through the Boston Ballet's Summer Program and living in a Boston University dorm. We'd been so excited when she received her acceptance letter! Allison had written several times telling me how much she was learning. I couldn't wait for her next letter. *If only Allison were here now*, I thought. *I'd feel less nervous.*

"I see it," I shouted, spotting the Wilton Drive sign partially hidden behind some pine trees.

A road wound gradually up a small hill. At the top stood an enormous, elegant three-story brick mansion with arched facades and spires similar to castles I'd seen in fairy tales and ballets, like *Sleeping Beauty*. The mansion commanded a dramatic view of the distant ocean. As we approached the mansion, rain splashed against the car windows. Wind whirled raindrops into a frantic dance as Dad stopped the car under the mansion's ivy-covered portico.

I pulled the hood of my raincoat tightly over my head, opened the car door and followed my parents to the large, beautifully-carved wooden door. The wind whipped my coat wildly and threw rain into my face.

Dad lifted the brass door knocker, banging it loudly. No one answered. After trying again, he slowly opened the heavy door. We entered a foyer with a Persian rug, a telephone and several long benches. No one was there. Dad put my suitcases down and said, "Stay here. I'll find the office." He disappeared through the door at the end of the foyer.

Soon he returned with a tall, middle-aged woman. Her shiny black hair was twisted into a neat French knot. She wore a long black dress and a beautiful, red and orange silk scarf wrapped around her neck. I immediately knew she'd been a ballerina from the graceful way she approached us. She extended her hand to Mom.

"It's nice to meet you, Mrs. Price. I'm Mrs. Weir, camp director."

Turning from Mom to me, she said, "You must be Jo. Welcome to Briar Point Ballet Camp. Mrs. Evans has told me all about you and the wonderful progress you've made in the last year." When she shook my hand, it was firm and business-like but her smile was genuine.

I felt a bit awkward, as if she were a queen to whom I should curtsy, but I only said, "Thanks."

"Come along. I'll show you the mansion."

Mrs. Weir led us through the inner door to a large, mahogany-paneled room with a three-story-high ceiling from which a crystal chandelier hung. Curving staircases, on either side of the room, led to a first-floor balcony. Another set of stairs led to a second-floor balcony. I saw one girl walking along the first-floor balcony and another one disappearing through a door.

"This is our main hall. Upstairs are the dormitories. Your room is on the third floor, Jo. We'll go there later. Mr. Price, please leave Jo's suitcases here by the stairs while I show you the rest of the mansion."

I'd never imagined the camp to be so large and ornate. I felt like I'd entered a dream. Mrs. Weir continued, "This house was built in the 1890s as a summer home for the Fordham family of New York City. They made their fortune during the booming shoe industry of the time. Originally, there were fifty-six rooms. The family required over thirty servants to work in the mansion and on its grounds. The mansion was named Chesterdale Manor after their two oldest sons. We simply call it the main house."

Mrs. Weir directed us to the right where we entered a large room filled with lounge chairs, tables, a couch, and a fire in a huge stone fireplace that threw off welcome heat. Bookcases filled two walls from floor to ceiling. A large picture window overlooked a deck that faced an enormous backyard.

"We have campfire nights by the fireplace when it's rainy and cold like today. The girls can come here during their free time to play cards or relax."

Exiting to our left, we passed a double door to the deck crowded with picnic tables. Two stone pillars stood at the top of a long stone staircase leading down to the yard.

Mrs. Weir brought us into another large room with many rows of long, narrow tables and chairs. "Here is the dining hall. The kitchen is in the back." I heard the banging of pots and pans and smelled chicken cooking. As we moved on, I heard footsteps above me and looked up. Noticing my reaction, Mrs. Weir explained, "On Sunday's we have quiet time in the late afternoon. It just ended so you're hearing the girls leaving their rooms. During the week quiet time is after lunch when the girls stay in their rooms to rest or write letters." Then, turning to my parents, she continued, "The girls have such active days we feel mandatory breaks are necessary and we have a ten o'clock lights-out rule."

"Sounds wise," replied Mom.

"Well, let's find your room, Jo. Your roommate is Julia Carmichael. She's from New York City and she's Briar Point's most talented ballerina. Mr. Price, would you mind waiting for us? Men aren't allowed upstairs."

"Of course not," Dad said, handing the suitcases to Mom and me.

We followed Mrs. Weir up two sets of stairs and across the balcony to a hallway. Off of it were many small rooms and one large bathroom with showers. We passed girls walking down the hall busily chatting. My room was at the end of the hall. A wide window on one wall faced the ocean. Julia's bed was neatly made. Next to it was an unmade bed with linens on it. To the right of Julia's bed stood a bureau and a floor-length mirror with newspaper clippings and photos of ballerinas carefully arranged around it.

"Julia must be in the shower or somewhere else. You'll meet her soon. Well, I'll leave you to say your goodbyes and get settled. Dinner is at 6 o'clock sharp." Then, to my mom, she said, "The girls are allowed to call home one night a week. Jo's day is Tuesday. We don't take calls from parents unless it's an emergency."

Suddenly I felt both excitement and loneliness blow through me, cold and damp like the weather. For the first time I thought about going back home, which was odd. I'd been obsessed about going to Briar Point Ballet Camp for the past month. My voice cracked a little as I said, "What if I need to call you before Tuesday, Mom?"

"Oh, for heaven's sake, Jo, it's only two days away. You'll be fine. Anyway, you can write us every day." I hated Mom's practical advice. I wanted her to hug me and say I could leave. Before I could protest, she added, "You're going to have a terrific time."

Would I? Why was I acting so childish and spoiled? After all, I was thirteen years old. Why couldn't I give things a chance? I looked at Mom. Reluctantly, I agreed.

After making the bed, we found Dad waiting for us in the foyer. "Are you all set?" he asked me. I nodded my head, afraid I'd cry if I spoke. "Good," Dad said. "We must leave before the storm gets worse. It's a long ride home."

At the door, I gave Mom a quick hug. I held onto Dad longer than usual, hoping he would sense my concerns. He didn't. I watched as they drove away, raindrops falling down the windowpane like the tears I wanted to shed.

Meeting Julia

Julia was not in the room when I returned. Alone, a dull ache began in my stomach, growing until it felt as if it were a stone. To calm myself, I unpacked my suitcase and put my clothes in the bureau. Outside, the wind relentlessly hurled rain along the grounds toward the ocean. I turned away. My clock read four-thirty, an hour and a half before dinner. Restless and curious, I studied the old newspaper clippings and photographs placed around Julia's mirror. All the photos were of the same prima ballerina wearing costumes from many different ballets. Maybe she was Julia's idol or teacher.

The door creaked open. I snapped my head around embarrassed to be staring at her pictures. Julia entered dressed in a bathrobe with a towel wrapped around her head. She was tall, thin and had a perfectly heart-shaped face, wide blue eyes and thin lips.

"Welcome to Briar Point Ballet Camp, the famous cultural camp of rural Maine. I'm Julia."

I couldn't tell if she was being sarcastic. "Hi, Julia. I'm Jo," I said as I moved toward my bed.

"I expected you around noon. When you didn't show, I thought you weren't coming."

"Oh, no, we arrived an hour ago. It's a five-hour drive from my home."

She turned around, unwrapped the towel and let down her long brown hair. An uncomfortable silence followed. I'd imagined a more friendly reception. None of my expectations about camp were coming true.

"How old are you, anyway?" she finally asked.

I thought this was an odd way to start a conversation. "I'm thirteen and I'm going into eighth grade. Why do you ask?"

"Oh, I just expected you'd be a lot older," she said, pulling a comb through her damp hair. "Where are you from?"

Staring at Julia's back, I said, "I'm from Durham, New Hampshire. Mrs. Weir said you're from New York City."

"Yes, I live in Manhattan, on the Upper East Side." Julia looked in her mirror as she meticulously twisted her hair into a tight bun.

"Oh," I said. I'd never been to New York City. Manhattan's Upper East Side meant nothing to me. "Do you like it there?"

"Love it. I wanted to stay in the city this summer, but my father insisted I get fresh air. I couldn't care less." I wondered what the city was like in the summer, probably hot, sticky, and dirty. Of course, I didn't say that. Julia continued, "I told Father that I *refuse* to come next year. I've been here five summers."

"You have?"

"Yes. The teachers are good but none of the dancers here are at my level. Serious ballet students stay in the city during the summer. This fall I'll be a junior in high school. So I'll be old enough to attend the summer dance program at the New York City Ballet. That's when the director picks talented ballet dancers to become apprentices to the company. Then they have the potential to become members of the <u>corps</u>. If I'm chosen, I'll quit school."

"You'll *quit*?" I was shocked.

"Sure. Lots of kids leave high school to become professional ballet dancers."

"They do?" I asked, eager to learn more.

Julia turned to face me. "Of course. *Everyone* knows that company directors and teachers look for new talent during their summer programs. They like molding young <u>corps</u> members into future ballerinas. I'm going to be one of them someday soon."

"What about your high school diploma?"

"Simple. Daddy will hire a tutor and I'll take the high school equivalency test."

"Oh."

I mulled over Julia's information as she disrobed and changed into sweatpants and a top. I felt extremely naïve compared to her, but I reminded myself that not everyone knows how ballet companies operate.

Julia interrupted my thoughts. "I've always had my own room," she stated. "I don't know why you're rooming with me."

"Who knows? Maybe it's because I'm starting camp in the middle of the summer."

"Probably. Anyway, you *better* respect my space, or I'll have you thrown out. Understand?"

Shocked, I hesitated before stating firmly, "I assume you'll respect my space, too."

Julia didn't answer. Obviously she'd had enough of me.

"I'm going to read. Then we'll go to dinner."

"OK," I said.

I lay down on my bed thinking how much Julia reminded me of Leslie Louise. There was one big difference, however. I have to *live* with Julia for the *whole month*.

In the dining hall she introduced me to the four girls at our table. They were politely curious. Where was I from? Where did I study ballet and for how long? The girls, all several years older than me, lived in the New York City area where they'd studied at professional ballet schools. All had taken toe classes for two or three years. I felt uncomfortably out of place telling them that I was from a small town and that I was not on pointe.

I was relieved when we were interrupted by the clatter of china and the savory smell of the chicken pie platter that was passed around with fresh salad and bread. Julia filled her plate with salad while the rest of us heaped on the chicken. It was delicious. As we ate, the girls talked among themselves, ignoring me. They reminded me of the popular girls at Oyster River Junior High who disliked me. Would I fit in here?

We'd almost finished eating when Mrs. Weir stood up to tap her glass for quiet. I feared she would introduce me before the entire camp. Instead, she announced that ice cream sundaes would be served in the lounge before the camp sing-along.

Julia showed me where to return my dirty dishes and we left for the lounge. A line had formed for the ice cream. Near the front stood a girl about my age with a cute turned-up nose and short brown hair. When she saw me, she smiled pleasantly.

Noticing this, Julia said, "That's Faye. She's from somewhere in Rhode Island. I don't know how she got accepted. She's terrible at ballet but I've heard she's a good jazz dancer."

I watched Faye scoop ice cream into her dish and join friends seated on the sofa, laughing. I wondered what was funny and longed to be with them.

Julia took a small amount of ice cream and waited for me to fill my dish. I followed her to a spot near the fireplace where we sat on the floor.

"Ice cream is my favorite. It's the only thing worth eating here," remarked Julia.

I wondered why she'd taken so little of her favorite food, but I only said, "Oh?"

"Yes, salads and ice cream. That's it."

We ate in silence until Julia asked, "Are you staying for the sing-along?"

"Yes. Why?"

"I'm going upstairs to finish my book."

"Fine," I said, grateful to be rid of her.

After Julia left, a woman handed out pages of folk song lyrics. We sang for the next two hours while she played her guitar. I relaxed completely, enjoying the music and the warmth from the fire. I felt happier than

I had all day. Camp was going to be fun. I felt sure of it until I returned to my room.

Julia was on the floor exercising. This was her daily routine, she said, promising to be done soon. I crawled into bed. It was almost ten-thirty before she shut the light off. *She really is crazy*, I thought as I succumbed to sleep.

The First Day

I awoke to warm sun on my face. Julia slept. I dressed quietly and looked out the window at a crystal-clear day. The ocean sparkled in the distance, an inviting royal blue, not the menacing dark blue-green of my dream. Things seemed hopeful again.

I heard a loud bell persistently ringing as I headed to the bathroom.

Julia stirred and groaned, "I hate that bell."

"What is it?"

"The wake-up bell. Breakfast is in half an hour."

"Oh, OK I'll be washing up."

"Fine."

When I returned, Julia had fallen back to sleep. Should I wake her? I wondered. No, I'll annoy her.

In the dining hall, I was pleased when Heather, one of the girls at my table, greeted me, warmly asking me how I'd enjoyed the sing-along. The scrambled eggs were being served when Julia arrived. We were eating when Mrs. Weir approached.

"How was your first night, Jo?"

"Very nice, thanks."

"Good. If you need anything, just ask." Then, turning to Julia, she said, "I'd like you to show Jo around the camp and take her to her classes." Julia's eyes narrowed and her mouth tightened. Mrs. Weir continued, "I've told your teacher that you'll be a bit late. She'll understand. Jo is on the level-2 schedule."

"But, Mrs. Weir, level-2 classes are in the carriage house ten minutes from Stonegate. I'll miss most of the barre."

"You'll be OK. It's only for today."

"But," Julia began.

Mrs. Weir gave her a stern look and walked away.

"I can find the classes on my own, Julia," I protested.

"No. Forget it. Mrs. Weir always gets her way. Come on. Put your dishes away and get your dance bag."

On our way to the carriage house, we passed a large swimming pool and beautifully manicured lawns still damp from yesterday's rain. We followed a gravel road into the woods. Girls leisurely walked ahead of us to their classes.

"Hurry," insisted Julia. "I could injure myself if I miss too much of the barre."

It's not my fault that Julia's irritated, I thought. I had offered to go by myself. She could be as upset as she liked. I wasn't rushing.

I knew Julia wanted to run but she had to keep my slower pace. As we walked, she explained that my mornings would be spent at the carriage house where my ballet classes and arts and crafts were both located. She said Mr. James Capp was my ballet teacher and Mrs. Marrisa Schneider was my arts and crafts teacher. Lunch and quiet time were next, followed by jazz class and sports at Stonegate, the stone building beside the main house. Then free time was before dinner.

"I don't know why Briar Point Ballet Camp has jazz classes. It's supposed to be a ballet camp *for heaven's sake*! My first year at camp, I *refused* to take jazz classes. I got special permission and haven't taken jazz since. Anyway, this afternoon we'll go to Stonegate," said Julia as we approached the carriage house.

Built in the same style as the main house, it hid among a grove of trees. Rust-colored paint peeled from around its windows and carriage door, but the inside featured a well-kept, modern dance studio with a large wooden floor, barres against its walls and screened-in windows. Pine scent and bird songs filled the room. It would be like dancing in the woods and I couldn't wait!

Mr. Capp, a man in his early thirties, greeted us. His thick black hair complimented his brown eyes and, although he was not a tall man, his physique was stunning. His arms were muscular, his torso tapered to a narrow waist and he stood perfectly erect, which made him appear tall. Mr. Capp was so handsome! I couldn't help staring at him. I'd never had a male ballet teacher, but I already liked him.

"Mr. Capp, this is Jo Price, my roommate. She just arrived yesterday."

He shook my hand firmly and smiled. "Welcome, Jo, pleased to meet you," he said in a surprisingly soft-spoken voice.

"Excuse me, Mr. Capp, but I've got to get to class," Julia said, bolting out the door.

After she left, Mr. Capp said, "Just do your best today. There may be new steps that you don't know. Don't worry. You're learn them soon enough."

I thanked him, scanned the studio and grew nervous when I didn't recognize anyone. Girls stood in groups chatting until Mr. Capp started the class. The familiar ballet barre put me at ease until the <u>développé</u> <u>a</u> <u>la</u> <u>seconde</u> exercise. From <u>passé</u>, I extended my leg to the side. It quivered in protest as I tried to lift it higher. Stay up, stay up, I silently urged it. Everyone's <u>développés</u> were much higher than mine. Suddenly, my leg slammed to the floor with a thud. Thankfully, no one noticed.

Mr. Capp abruptly stopped the music. "No, no, no, ladies," he shouted, his previously soft-spoken voice gone. "Keep your hips even. No hip-tilting to show off a high développé. This is cheating. It's dangerous. Repeating bad habits causes injuries. Watch as I extend my leg while keeping my hip down." Without holding the barre, Mr. Capp moved his working leg to passé, lifted his knee up, and then extended his lower leg. His hips had not tilted. Back at the record player, he said, "Now, try again."

Later, Mr. Capp grouped us for the center floor work. He placed me in the last group so I could practice the combinations at the back of the room before my group was called. During an adagio combination, we repeated the dreaded développé. Although my legs did not extend very high, and they trembled, I knew I'd done my best. During the allegro combinations, however, I couldn't keep up with the tempo. I felt like a clown flopping over my own feet.

After the class, I approached Mr. Capp, who gave me another friendly smile. "I think Mrs. Weir should have put me in the level-1 class. I can't keep up."

"Don't be silly. You're in the right place. Give yourself credit. This is only your first class and I see you have potential. Your dancing will improve."

I thanked him, blushed and left to change clothes for arts and crafts. At the arts and crafts studio, on the other side of the carriage house, I met Mrs. Schneider. She was a small, wiry woman with curly red hair. Mrs. Schneider taught me to wedge clay while everyone laughed and joked as they worked on their hand-built pottery pieces.

I am alone again, I thought, as I trudged back to the main house after arts and crafts. Why was this happening? I'd daydreamed about Briar Point Ballet Camp ever since I'd received the scholarship. In my imagination, the girls at camp had been friendly. In reality, they weren't. Memories of Laura's rotten attitude and the loss of her friendship crept into my mind. Would the girls here judge me on my looks? Would they be as nasty as the popular girls at Oyster River Junior High?

My stomach clenched as I entered the dining hall. Heather, Julia, and the other girls, chatting with each other, ignored me when I sat down. I stared at the macaroni and cheese on my plate. Suddenly, I wasn't hungry. I forced myself to take a few bites, and then I returned my tray.

Back in my room, quiet time was almost over when Julia closed her book and turned to me. "I'm sorry I rushed you this morning. I hate missing the barre 'cause I can't warm up properly. Also, I like sticking to my schedule."

Maybe Julia's apology meant she wouldn't be as mean-spirited as Laura or Leslie Louise after all. "It's OK. I understand. It was odd, though. Why did Mrs. Weir insist on having you come with me to the carriage house?"

"She wanted you properly introduced to Mr. Capp. Mrs. Weir is strange about certain things and strict with the rules. Did you know that during quiet time we can't play radios, visit friends, or make any noise? She treats us like children."

"Really? What if you're noisy?"

"She'll take away the camp store privilege. You can buy candy bars, ice cream sandwiches, and other goodies there. Or Mrs. Weir might take away an evening event. But she's particularly strict with the rules about leaving camp. Last year one girl forgot to sign out at free time. She went into town and was late to dinner. Mrs. Weir kept her from attending the next dance at the boys' camp. So, no one wants to break important rules or, if they do, they're careful."

"I see. I didn't know there were social dances. Are they for level-2 girls?"

"Sure. Everyone goes if they want. There are two more scheduled this summer."

Julia got up, stuffed her toe shoes into her bag and put on her tights. I heard doors banging and voices in the hall. Quiet time was over. So, I dressed for the jazz class and we walked the short distance to Stonegate. It consisted of a dance studio and a recreation hall. The rec hall, as it was called, was used at free time and for sports during bad weather.

In the dance studio, Miss Summers, a middle-aged woman, was dancing to Duke Ellington's music. She moved quickly to the beat, causing her long, black hair to fling loosely about, as her body formed interesting angular shapes. She stopped when she saw us, shut off the record and bounded toward us as if she had more energy than her little body could contain.

"Hi, Julia. What a nice surprise. Coming for a jazz

class?" Before Julia could answer, she faced me. "I'd love her to take a jazz class, but she's stuck on ballet."

"Sorry, Miss Summers. I'm not here for class. This is my new roommate, Jo Price. I'm showing her to her classes."

"Pleased to meet you, Jo. Mrs. Weir said you'd be joining us. I understand you've never taken a jazz class. That's not a problem. Just follow along the best you can. Jazz, as you know, is very different from ballet. Remember we're here to have fun."

"I'll try." I liked her relaxed attitude.

Then Julia said, "I've got to go. See you at dinner, Jo."

Before the class started, Miss Summers introduced me and had each girl say her name. Faye, who I remembered from the night before, was there. Next, Miss Summers demonstrated the warm-up exercises in the middle of the room. Beside Faye, who smiled broadly at me, stood a tall girl wearing bright pink shorts and a pink and black polka-dotted top. It seemed odd seeing different colored leotards, shorts and tank tops instead of the typical ballet-pink tights and black leotards.

Although I enjoyed the class, the jazz steps were awkward, fast, and I felt foolish attempting them. After class, Miss Summers praised me. Although I knew she was lying, I smiled gratefully. She explained that jazz is a different dance language from ballet but that, with repetition, I would learn it. I'd never thought of dance as a language before. I pondered this as I left for sports.

In the rec hall, everyone picked up bows and arrows

and went outside to practice archery. I had no interest in shooting an arrow. I hit the target only a few times but loved being on the enormous field that spread out from the back deck of the main house. After returning my equipment, I headed to my room. Free time loomed ahead. What would I do? Where would I go? Everyone had left. I was alone.

Homesickness

I walked toward the main house. The sun shined brightly through the foliage, a green mosaic against the blue sky. Ahead of me a group of girls giggled, sang and skipped along the path. I sat under a tree feeling sullen and watched them disappear into the main house.

I hated those giggling girls. They reminded me of mean girls who'd laughed at me in the past. I felt as if I were in the middle of the ocean with no one in sight, starting to sink. My ocean dream must have been an *omen*, I reasoned. I shouldn't have come.

An ache moved across my forehead. I tried to push it away, unsuccessfully. It moved relentlessly into a tension headache. A huge lump formed in my throat. Tears welled up in my eyes. I fiercely wiped them away, determined to act grown-up.

My grandfather once quoted Abraham Lincoln, who said, "Most folks are about as happy as they make up their minds to be." How could I *make up my mind* to be happy? Did I really have a choice? I wondered. I stood up and returned to my room. Thankfully, Julia wasn't there. I sat on my bed and wrote to my parents.

August 2, 1960
Dear Mom and Dad,
    I HATE camp. My roommate is strange.
She's not very friendly and nobody else is
either.
    I want to go home. Please come and get
me as
    soon as possible. I can't stay here any
longer.
    I miss you terribly.
    Love, Jo

I addressed, stamped, sealed the envelope and start-ed to bawl. Finally, exhausted, I fell on my pillow and slept until the dinner bell rang.

That evening, girls shared candy, popcorn, and Cokes with their friends while Mr. Weir, a distin-guished-looking gentleman with a goatee and a small pot belly, set up a projector to show the movie *The Red Shoes*. I was finally going to see the famous movie! Julia sat on the other side of the room. I sat alone.

Back in our room, Julia began doing abdominal crunches. This time I asked why she needed to exercise after dancing for hours in ballet classes. She said she needed to lose weight. I stated that she was the thinnest girl at camp. Julia refused to believe me, which con-vinced me that she was even crazier than I thought.

Irritated, I climbed into bed and pulled the blanket over my head. Then, remembered Mrs. Weir's lights-out rule, I mentioned this to Julia. She scoffed at this and said no one obeyed the rule. By eleven o'clock, she was still puffing and moaning. I was fed up. Why had I waited this long to complain? I sprang from my bed. My head ached. "I'm shutting the lights *off*. I can't sleep."

"Only five more minutes and I'm done."

I stormed to the bathroom, fury growing with each footstep.

That was it. I wanted a new roommate, I decided. Tomorrow I'd speak with Mrs. Weir.

The next morning I awoke to a gentle breeze playing with the curtains. They looked like angel wings moving the sunlight around the room. Once again, a positive attitude overtook me. But it didn't last. My dance classes were terrific, and my other activities were OK. However, I grew increasingly lonely and too depressed to speak with Mrs. Weir about Julia. Maybe going home was the answer.

That night, waiting in the foyer to call my parents, I heard the girl ahead of me talking and laughing on the telephone. How could she be so happy when I was so miserable? Finally, I heard the click of the phone.

"It's all yours," she said, her face glowing.

I dialed the number. Three rings. Four rings. Someone answer, *please*.

"Hello."

"Mom..." My throat closed up.

"Jo, are you there?"

"Yes," I managed to say, my voice wavering. "I want to go home." I began to wail.

"Calm down. What's wrong?"

My heartbeat and breathing slowed slightly. Between gasps of air I told her how unfriendly everyone was and that Julia was keeping me awake.

"What did you do about it?"

"I talked with her but it didn't help. I want to go home. When can you come?"

"You've got to work things out, Honey. You've only been at camp a few days. Give it some more time."

"More time! I can't, Mom."

"What's stopping you?"

What's stopping me? How dumb was she?

"I just told you."

"Well, think a minute. What else can you do?"

Why did Mom always ask questions when I needed answers?

"I don't know. I thought about asking Mrs. Weir for a different roommate."

"Why didn't you?"

"She probably won't let me," I said, skirting the real issue that I felt too emotional to handle it.

"It's worth a try, isn't it?"

"I guess so."

"Your dad's at a meeting but he sends his love." Mom was ending our conversation. Any hope of returning home was gone. "We love you. I'm sure things will be better when you call next week."

I wanted to say, "*Sure,* Mom. Thanks for *nothing.*" Instead, I simply said goodbye.

I sat staring at the phone realizing that nothing

would change unless I spoke to Mrs. Weir. With a sudden burst of energy, I went to her office and knocked on the door. Surprised, she looked up from her paperwork.

"Oh, Jo, hi. What can I do for you?"

"May I speak with you?'

"Certainly." She got up, closed the door and returned to her seat. "Please sit down. Tell me what's bothering you."

I could smell her Shalimar Perfume and see the concern on her face. I wondered how to begin.

"I want to switch roommates," I blurted out.

"You do? Aren't you and Julia getting along? She's Briar Point's most talented ballerina, you know."

What does that have to do with it? She's a lousy roommate, I wanted to say. Instead I explained, "Julia's been exercising late at night, keeping me up."

"Have you spoken with her?"

"Yes, but she refuses to stop. Besides she hardly speaks to me."

"Julia has always roomed alone and she's an only child who never had to compromise. Now she needs to learn. Tell her I insist she follow the lights-out rule and that she stop exercising. Julia's talented and thin enough."

"Me? You want *me* to tell her?" Why did I have to handle it? Wasn't it Mrs. Weir's job? Then, more boldly, I asked, "Isn't there someone else I could room with?"

"Sorry, we don't switch roommates once they are assigned." It sounded so final. "Good luck. You'll work things out. If you have other concerns, please see me again."

Highly unlikely, I thought as I opened the door to leave. I turned back and smiled pleasantly, though I was thoroughly miffed, and muttered, "Thank you."

I walked outside to the deck and sat at a picnic table to think things over. Both Mrs. Weir and Mom wanted me to confront Julia again. But would she compromise?

The Confrontation

That night, Julia exercised until almost eleven o'clock again. When she finally turned out the light, I fell into a fitful sleep. I dreamt I'd fallen off my bicycle. Lying in the dirt by the roadside, I kept screaming for help from Mom and Mrs. Weir but they weren't around.

When I awoke the next morning, I thought about confronting Julia. I would confront her the same way I had confronted Laura when she'd befriended Leslie Louise. I would state the facts and my feelings about them.

At quiet time, I turned to Julia and simply said, "I'm really upset."

Julia looked up from her book, set it down and gave me an inquisitive look. Was it surprise or concern? I wasn't sure. "What's wrong?"

"I'm angry that you've kept me awake for the last three nights." When she said nothing, I continued, "I asked Mrs. Weir for a new roommate but she refused. She said you need to compromise."

Julia looked hurt. "You told her you didn't want to room with me?"

"Yes. You aren't being considerate of my needs." There, I'd said it!

"I'm sorry, Jo. Really I am. You're right. I've been

selfish. I'll exercise during evening events so I won't keep you awake."

"Fine," I said, thinking our discussion was over, but Julia continued.

"A ballerina is never talented enough. There's always a better dancer waiting to take your place. That's why I exercise. Besides, my ballet teacher in New York City told me to watch my weight. Only thin dancers are accepted into companies." Julia paused, took one of the newspaper clippings from her mirror, handed it to me and continued, "Someday I'm going to look like my mother." When I looked at it, shock must have registered on my face because Julia said, "Yes, she was my mother."

Puzzled, I asked, "Really? What do you mean? She *was* your mother?"

"She died in a car accident when I was nine. I was in the car, but I wasn't seriously injured."

"Oh, no, how terrible." The thought of losing Mom was beyond comprehension. Death happened in old age, not before.

Tears formed in Julia's eyes. She bit her lip and looked down. "It was devastating."

"I'm sorry."

"I can't talk about it anymore," she said, speaking so softly I could hardly hear her.

I wanted to console her, but I felt uncomfortable, filled with too many mixed emotions.

Instead, I said, "I understand." But did I? How could I understand the depth of her pain? My mind flooded with questions. Who had cared for her? What was it like without her mother? There was a terribly long pause before I could speak. I wasn't sure if Julia would talk about her mother's life, but I took the chance. "Was your mother a prima ballerina?"

"She was a principal dancer with the American Ballet Theatre before I was born."

I studied the clipping again, then handed it back to her.

"Wasn't she beautiful? See how petite she was, not like me. I take after my father, big-boned and heavy."

"How did your parents meet?" I inquired.

"My dad sold dancewear and fabrics to the ballet company. Then he was drafted into the army during World War II. They married when he was on leave. I was born right after he returned from the war. Mom had to stop dancing to care for me. She loved me but resented stopping. She wanted me to be the ballerina she'd once been."

Julia's life was extremely complicated. No wonder she acted strangely.

Noises in the hall brought me back to the present. Quiet time was over. We began preparing for our classes.

"Please don't tell anyone about my mother. I don't like to discuss it."

"Of course not," I replied.

As I dressed, I thought about our conversation. I was relieved Julia had compromised and changed her exercise time. Maybe things between us would work out. I felt proud of myself. I'd confronted her!

Making Friends

Later, after the evening event, I found Julia exercising. Seeing me, she got up from the floor and started preparing for bed.

"How was the storyteller?" she asked.

"Excellent. By the way, Mrs. Weir asked about you. I told her we'd worked things out."

"Great. From now on, if she asks why I'm not at the evening event, please tell her I'm knitting or reading. She mustn't know I'm exercising. She'll make me stop."

Immediately I felt uncomfortable. Julia wanted me to lie. How would I respond if Mrs. Weir asked about Julia again?

Lying in bed, I imagined different scenarios in which Mrs. Weir asked why Julia kept missing evening events. Since I'd never lied to an adult, I couldn't keep my anxiety at bay. Finally, I told myself to stop worrying. Mrs. Weir might never ask about Julia. This thought helped me slowly drift into sleep.

❧

On Wednesday afternoons, the dance studios were open during free time. So I decided to go to the carriage house to practice Miss Summer's jazz routines. During jazz class, I'd struggled with the foreign movements and the fast pace of the choreography. But, my real motivation for practicing at the carriage house was the possibility of seeing Mr. Capp who lived above the studio. I adored him. He was so patient and always gave positive suggestions. Naturally, I did my best to please him. The other day he held my hand as I bent forward in a <u>penché</u> <u>arabesque</u>. His touch sent energy, unnerving yet pleasant, tingling through my body, a touch different from any other and, when I glanced into his kind brown eyes, I felt a glow. For the last few days, I've watched him during class, at mealtimes and at evening events. I've even imagined myself sitting beside him. He holds my hand, smiles and tells me he likes me. He's an adult man, for heaven's sake. *I knew* I shouldn't feel this way, but I couldn't help it.

Mr. Capp wasn't at the carriage house studio but Faye, the girl I'd noticed my first night at camp, was there practicing pirouettes. I recalled Julia's description of her as a good jazz dancer with poor ballet skills. I'd watched Faye during our jazz class and admired her. She radiated pure joy as she moved. Slightly chubby, Faye didn't have a typical petite ballet body and, unlike most dancers who forced their long hair into tight buns, she let her short hair fly freely about her face. Faye stopped practicing her turns, cocked her head, and said, "Hi, Jo. What's up?"

I smiled at her, amazed that Faye had remembered my name. "I came to practice the jazz piece. Will I be in your way?"

"Not at all," she said.

I donned my shoes, danced awkwardly through the first part of the routine and stopped.

I turned to Faye, "Will you help me? I can't remember the rest of the jazz routine."

"Sure. I was just leaving but my friend won't mind if I'm a few minutes late. The next step is a jazz square. It goes like this." She watched me in the mirror as I copied her, and said, "Good, now this step is a mambo." Her hips swayed easily up and down but mine didn't. She started giggling. "You ballerinas don't know how to move your hips, do you?! Bend your knees and then try." When I did it, she clapped her hands. "You're getting it."

We'd been practicing for half an hour when a tall, lanky dancer bounced into the studio like a basketball bouncing onto a court. I'd often seen her with Faye. She wore a polka-dotted outfit like the one she'd worn during my first jazz class.

"I've been looking all over for you," she said, irritation evident as she spoke to Faye. "I thought we were going to see Dylan this afternoon."

"Oh, no! I completely forgot."

"It's my fault," I said. "Faye stayed to help me learn the jazz piece."

"Cece, this is Jo. Jo, Cece. We got so involved that I lost track of the time, sorry."

Cece stared at me, and then said, "Hi, I'm Cecilia Waters, Cece for short. I know you; you're the new girl in Miss Summers' class."

"Yes, I came a few days ago."

"Nice to meet you." Then, turning to Faye, she said in a less agitated tone. "What about seeing Dylan?"

"Let's go tomorrow. We won't be back in time for dinner if we leave now."

"I thought campers weren't allowed to be with boys off campgrounds," I interrupted.

They started laughing.

"Dylan is a horse! Cece is horse-crazy and boy-crazy. She rides Dylan at the stables near here. We have to wait for our next social dance to boy-watch."

"When's the dance?" I asked.

"Not soon enough," said Cece. "Actually, it's in six more days. But who's counting? I'm dying to see Stefan again. He's *so* handsome, Jo. Wait until you see him. Everyone wants to dance with him."

"Everyone, except Julia. She hasn't gone to any of the social dances. Julia always has some excuse. She's your roommate, right?" asked Faye.

"Yes. Why doesn't she go?"

"Who knows? She's a bit strange; she keeps to herself."

Thank goodness someone else thinks she's strange, I thought.

Then Cece asked, "How is it rooming with Briar Point's best ballerina?"

I was surprised by her question. I didn't want to discuss my roommate issues until I knew Cece better. So I said, "We're working things out."

"I bet you have lots to work out with her. She's used to having everything her own way, a real prima donna."

Hearing Cece say this made me feel better. Not everyone thought Julia was a perfect person simply because she was a talented ballet dancer.

As we walked back to the main house, I told Faye and Cece about my family and my ballet experiences. Cece told me she lived in a suburb of Denver, Colorado where she divided her free time between horse riding and dance. Faye lived in Rhode Island and took jazz classes. Her teacher had recommended that she attend camp to get some professional ballet training. Faye wanted to be a dance teacher. I was surprised to learn she wanted to teach. I assumed everyone at camp wanted to perform in a ballet company. Faye and Cece, like me, weren't from the New York City area and hadn't studied in professional ballet schools.

At the main house, when we were ready to return to our rooms, Faye asked if I wanted to play cards with Cece and her after dinner. I accepted her invitation immediately and felt happiness shine through me like sunlight sparkling on water.

Back in my room, I asked Julia about the next social dance. She said it would be held at the Rockhaven Boy Scout Camp in Springhill, about half an hour away. Julia mentioned that she'd been sick during the last dance. Due to her look, and from what Cece and Faye had told me, I didn't ask any questions. But I wondered. What was Julia's real reason for not going?

Mischief

Dear Mom and Dad,
I love camp and want to stay! A few days ago, I met two new friends, Faye and Cece. They are really nice, lots of fun! Even things with Julia are a bit better. I talked with her and told her that she was being inconsiderate. Julia even apologized! Now, at least, she isn't keeping me awake.
We've started learning the choreography to a Mozart piece that we will perform for parents at the end of camp. Yikes, the time is going so fast.
Love, Jo

I put my pen down and reread my letter. *Amazing*, I thought, *my loneliness has vanished*. I hated to admit that Mom was right when she said things would get better.

The dinner bell rang. I stopped writing and shoved my letter into an envelope so Julia wouldn't see it. I would seal the envelope, stamp and mail it tomorrow.

৯৵

A few days later, just before quiet time, Faye and I visited Cece's room. Above her bureau were photos of horses. I took one down, a photo Faye had taken of Cece on Dylan, a brown and white spotted horse with a beautiful brown mane. After putting it back, I admired a photo of Cece on a horse as he jumped over a fence. Flame, she said, was her favorite horse from home and a natural jumper. She'd won several Colorado state trophies riding him.

"Cece's as crazy over Flame and Dylan as I am over Mr. Capp."

Faye had mentioned her crush on Mr. Capp one evening while we played cards. That night, she'd pierced my daydreams, like a pin popping a balloon, sputtering and collapsing with each word she spoke. Why had I been so naïve? Other girls were crazy about him just like me. Nonetheless, my obsession with Mr. Capp hadn't stopped. I continued to think of our relationship as special, but I never told Faye.

"Yup, I'm crazy over horses and boys. She's crazy over one man." Cece laughed, and then asked, "Did you hear Mr. Capp has asked your famous roommate, Julia, to tutor Faye on the ballet piece for the final show?"

"Really?" I studied Faye's face. How did she feel? Before I could ask, she nodded her head slowly.

"Don't remind me! Julia starts tutoring me tomorrow at free time. I wish Mr. Capp had picked someone else."

"Too bad *he* isn't helping you," I said.

"Oh, how I wish!"

Looking at me with a mischievous grin, Cece said, "You need help from Mr. Capp, too. Don't you?"

Somehow she must have guessed about my crush. "He can't have favorites," I snapped. "It wouldn't be fair." But I didn't want to imagine Mr. Capp holding Faye's hand during her level-1 ballet class.

"My crush on Mr. Capp is too much to bear," declared Faye, acting overly dramatic as she pressed her hand to her forehead, pretending to faint. "I'm dying to see him any way I can."

"Hey, guess what?! He's meeting Miss Summers right now at the carriage house to discuss the order of dances for the performance," said Cece. "I overheard him speaking about it with Mrs. Weir a few minutes ago at lunch."

"Wow, perfect. Let's go make a visit. We'll sneak up on them and eavesdrop," declared Faye.

"But we can't," I told them, sounding like a prude. "Quiet time starts soon. Julia said Mrs. Weir takes privileges away if we're caught breaking rules."

"Oh, come on, Jo. Nobody checks on us," coaxed Cece.

"Don't worry. We've broken rules plenty of times and not been caught. Mrs. Weir only keeps that rule to satisfy our parents," added Faye.

What should I do? Part of me wanted to follow the rules but I was so obsessed with Mr. Capp that I wanted to see him at any cost. I didn't hesitate long. My heart pounding loudly, I said, "OK. Let's go."

After checking the hallway, we slipped out the back

door, down the fire escape, and then ran to the Carriage House, where we crept up to the windows. No one was in the studio. But we heard muffled voices upstairs. Cece started creeping up the outside stairs when we heard Mr. Capp's door creak open. Instantly, she fled down the stairs, following us as we raced to the main house, panting. We never looked back. Breathless, we climbed the fire escape, cautiously entered the hall, and tiptoed to our rooms.

When I opened my door, Julia frowned.

"What happened?" she demanded. "Mrs. Weir was looking for you. Here." She handed me a letter from my father, which I stuck under my pillow to read later. "She wanted to know where you were."

Oh, no! I'm going to lose a privilege and Mrs. Weir will tell my parents. I groaned. Julia continued, "I told her you were in the bathroom, not feeling well, and that I'd give you the letter. Where were you, anyway?"

I stared at Julia in silence and gratitude. "I was uh...outside and lost track of the time." She gave me an incredulous look, which I ignored. "Thanks a lot. I *really, really* appreciate that you covered for me."

"No sweat," she said and began reading her book.

During the remaining minutes of quiet time, I thought about Julia helping Faye with her level-1 ballet piece. Lately, like Faye, I'd been struggling with Mr. Capp's choreography for the final performance. Although my ballet skills weren't as good as my peers in the level-2 class, it hadn't bothered me at first. Because I'd joined mid-summer, Mr. Capp hadn't expected me to keep up. So, I'd kept my expectations realistic, learned loads of new steps and gained muscle strength. However, I'd begun berating myself for not yet mastering the allegro section.

Suddenly, I heard doors opening and slamming shut. Quiet time was over. I let my anxiety over the ballet piece go while I prepared for the rest of my day.

Keeping Secrets

The clear blue sky was full of puffy white clouds. It was miserably hot, close to ninety-five degrees. I felt sticky, sweaty, and uncomfortable after playing tennis. Faye, Cece, and I were returning our gym equipment when Cece suggested swimming at free time. I was a terrible swimmer. At the Durham Public Pool, I'd flunked the intermediate swimming tests, and I hated to put my head underwater. I usually didn't enjoy swimming but cool water sounded extremely inviting.

Before I could speak, Faye said, "I wish I didn't have practice today. I think I'll tell Julia I'm not feeling well and join you."

"Why not?" asked Cece. She turned to me, "Are you coming?"

I hesitated, and then said, "Sure." I hoped I didn't sound nervous. My ocean dream had drifted back into my consciousness. How safe would I be in the pool's deep end? Maybe my dream was an omen about swimming in the pool. I wrestled with the thought. Maybe the dream simply represented my fears about leaving home. I didn't know or care. I just wanted to cool off.

While Faye went to the carriage house to cancel her practice time, Cece and I returned to the main house, changed and walked to the swimming pool. I gingerly moved into the shallow end of the pool. Initially cold, the water was wonderfully refreshing, and grew slightly warmer as I moved. I floated on my back thinking about my swimming skills. Next year I would have to repeat intermediate swimming while everyone else my age qualified for advanced swimming or lifesaving. My legs, although strong in ballet class, became dead weights in the water. After swimming one length of the Durham Public Pool, I was exhausted.

Splash! Cece dove into the deep end, swam underwater, and popped up beside me like a seal, sleek and comfortable in the water, her long brown hair pressed smoothly against her head.

"Race you to the diving board," she challenged me.

I twisted onto my stomach and put my feet down. "No, thanks."

"Ah, come on. It's not far."

Again, I hesitated. "It's not that."

"What's wrong?" probed Cece. "You can tell me."

I looked into my friend's concerned eyes and said truthfully, "I'm afraid of deep water. I must touch the bottom or I'm terrified." I hoped this would end the discussion.

Cece's face, usually cheerful, took on a serious look that I hadn't seen before. She mulled my concerns over and then announced, "I have it. How about a float? It will keep you up and I'll swim beside you. I've passed lifesaving."

I considered this. Would a float help me relax so I

could swim in the deep end of the pool? Attempting to sound positive, I said, "OK, let's give it a try."

"Great," Cece exclaimed, climbing out of the water. "It won't be that scary, promise." She passed a group of girls lounging by the pool house, went in, and returned with a float that she handed to me. I slid part of it under my chest, held the sides, and kicked. With Cece beside me, I moved cautiously into the deep end.

"Keep going. You can do it," she encouraged.

I kicked my legs with as much strength as I could muster, moving steadily toward the side of the diving board. When I finally got there, I rested on the float, let my feet hang down and, to my great relief, began to enjoy myself. I swam with the float while Cece swam around or dove under me.

We had dried off and were lying on our towels when Faye joined us.

"Was Julia terribly upset?" Cece asked.

"You bet. I expected that, but I didn't think she'd be so rude. Julia called me a lousy ballet dancer and said I couldn't afford to be lazy if I wanted to be a ballerina."

"You're just not as perfect or as disciplined. That's why she's Briar Point's best ballerina. Me, I'd rather not work that hard. How do you tolerate rooming with Julia?" Cece asked me.

"It's not easy," I admitted. "Her life's complicated. Julia has lots of personal issues."

"Oh, like what?" inquired Cece.

Why had I mentioned Julia's personal problems? Would I betray her trust? Feeling like a snake slithering away from a predator, I decided I could not. Instead I stated, "I can't talk about it."

"I'm dying to know her problems, being the nosey person that I am, but I respect you for not telling," said Cece.

"I agree," added Faye. "Let's forget her. I'm anxious to get into the pool."

♋

The social dance at the boys' camp was only a few days away. Everyone was talking about it, everyone but Julia. Would she pretend to be sick again? Finally, my curiosity took over. I asked her if she was going.

"No. I'm staying here."

"Why?"

"If I tell you, it's going to sound silly so it's our secret, OK?" she asked, nervously fingering her bracelet.

"OK, but what do you mean?"

She sighed deeply and stared out the window. "I don't want to meet a boy and fall in love. I'm not messing up my career like my mother."

"That's not silly. *It's utterly ridiculous!* You're not going to marry the first boy who asks you to dance. You'll probably never see him again," I insisted.

When she turned to face me, she was biting her lower lip. "I know, but I'm not taking a chance. Some girls fall in love, marry their high school sweethearts, get pregnant, and never have a career."

Julia had made her decision. I couldn't change what

she thought or did. I realized it was useless encouraging her to go to the dance.

Instead, I focused on myself, hoping desperately to have fun at the dance. This would be a new chance, if I could keep negative memories from Oyster River Junior High social dances away.

❧❧

Several days later, Faye, pretending to be a contestant in the Miss America Beauty Pageant, walked gracefully between the two beds in her room, imagining herself walking down the runway. She turned slowly, modeling the dress she would wear to the dance.

"Ladies and gentlemen, please welcome Miss Rhode Island. Isn't her lavender gown stunning? Notice the low-cut neckline and the sequins," announced Cece, acting as the host of the TV show. After we clapped for Faye, Cece remarked, "I can't wait to dance with Stefan and stare into his big, gorgeous brown eyes again. I just know he wanted to kiss me at the last dance. So, Miss Rhode Island, don't make any plans 'cause he's mine."

Faye twirled around, her joyful expression gone. "Let's change the subject, shall we?"

I'd never seen her so upset with Cece. I wondered what was behind Faye's anger. Although curious, I decided not to get involved or ask questions. If I did, it would be like putting my nose in a beehive where I might get stung.

"Is Julia going to the dance?" asked Faye after she'd

taken off her dress.

"No," I said.

"Why not?" asked Cece. "She'd be popular with the boys."

"I don't know," I lied.

"Didn't she give you a reason?"

"No, she just said she wasn't going," I lied again.

"I'm surprised she didn't say anything."

Cece was nosey and in a strange mood. Suddenly I didn't want to be around her. I told Faye and her that I needed a shower and left before they could ask any more questions. Knowing and keeping Julia's secrets had its difficulties.

I stopped at the window in the top-floor hallway that overlooked the ocean. I was glad to forget Julia's issues and my friends' spat. The sun sparkling across the deep blue-green water, a necklace of crystals scattered along the horizon. With my happy mood restored, I continued down the hall. I hadn't thought about my depressing ocean dream in days.

Stefan

The bus sped along the coastline to the social dance at the boys' camp. The early evening sun spread its pleasant warmth. A cool ocean breeze tossed my shoulder-length hair gently around my head.

"There it is," announced Cece, pointing to a group of buildings that hugged a beautiful rocky cove. "I hope Stefan asks me to dance. If he doesn't, I'm asking him even before ladies' choice."

She's got nerve! I thought. Nobody does that. In Durham, girls waited for the disc jockey to announce ladies' choice. I hated ladies' choice. I didn't want to ask a boy to dance with me. He might say no, too embarrassed to dance with me due to my birth defect. Instead, I would wait all night for some nice boy to ask for a dance. It never happened. Finally, I stopped going to Oyster River Junior High social dances. Tonight, I tried reminding myself this dance could be different. But, would it?

The boys' camp consisted of small brown cabins hidden among the jack pines. In addition, a clubhouse and a lodge, with an attached boathouse, were located in front of the cove and its small pebbly beach. A sailboat was tied to a wharf and several rowboats sat idly on the shore.

The bus stopped at the clubhouse where we got off. Mr. Harkman, a middle-aged man in a senior scout uniform and the camp director, spoke briefly with Mrs. Weir and Miss Summers, our chaperones for the evening, and then welcomed us. We followed him through the clubhouse into the lodge, a large room decorated with colored lights hung from the ceiling. Near the back of the room a man was adjusting a microphone. He stood in front of a long table holding a stack of 45-speed records and a record player with two large-sized speakers.

Cece led Faye and me to a table and chairs. When the boys arrived, they clustered together, chatted among themselves, surveying us from the opposite side of the room. Again, I recalled the dreadful dances I'd experienced. Why couldn't I keep those awful thoughts away? The popular girls at Oyster River Junior High, like my former friend, Laura, were always asked to dance. At the end of the night, I usually danced one dance with Timmy Soma. He greased his hair with Brylcreem and his fingernails were dirty from working at his father's garage station. Invariably he'd step on my toes. I was humiliated.

"There he is!" exclaimed Cece, pointing to a boy with black hair, brown eyes and a pleasant smile. "See, didn't I tell you he was handsome?" Stefan was dressed casually in a dark-green polo shirt and brown slacks. With his arms crossed, he stood tapping his foot slightly as if nervous or bored. He was handsome; I had to agree. Cece continued, "He's not getting away from me this time. Want to bet on it? I'm going to freshen up my lipstick. Back in a minute." She smoothed out her shocking-red satin skirt, picked up her purse and headed for the ladies' room.

Faye turned to me and said, "She's more boy-crazy than ever! I hope Stefan doesn't ask me to dance like he did at the last dance. Cece was *so upset*. She also hated the fact that I danced with more boys. Imagine...she was actually counting them."

It was hard to imagine Cece acting so childish. But, when it came to boys, she was a different person. Before I could ask any questions, I heard Cece's high heels clicking as she approached us.

In a few minutes, the disc jockey picked up the microphone and announced the first dance would be to a fast rock and roll song.

Right away Faye and Cece were asked to dance. I watched enviously as they danced several dances in a row. I noticed that Stefan wasn't among the boys. He hadn't asked Cece or anyone else to dance. Instead, he walked back and forth from the refreshment table, drinking Coke and watching the couples dance. Why didn't he ask Cece to dance? Maybe he didn't like her as much as she thought.

Between dances Cece complained that Stefan was ignoring her. So, when the first slow dance began, she marched over to him and asked him to dance. Although he appeared surprised because ladies' choice had not been called, he took her into his arms and waltzed her gracefully about the room. After the dance, he thanked her but didn't invite her to dance again.

I hadn't had one dance, not one lousy dance. Standing alone waiting at the side of the room, I feared that, once again, my birth defect was keeping boys from dancing with me. I hadn't thought about my drooping left eyelid very much since I'd come to camp. Now, old feelings of self-pity rose up like memories from a bad dream. No, I reminded myself; those feelings would not haunt me. Deep down I knew my self-worth didn't depend upon my physical appearance, my popularity, or lack of it. No one could take my self-worth away unless

I let them, not even Laura, Leslie Louise, or their popular friends. Now, I ached for one dance, just one, before the night was over.

My head began to ache. This social was no different from the ones at home. I looked at my watch. An hour had passed and the disc jockey wasn't stopping for a break.

I couldn't stand feeling miserable a minute longer. Faye and Cece were dancing. Mrs. Weir and Miss Summers were standing near the disc jockey, their backs to me, chatting with the man who'd first welcomed us. Keeping my eyes on them, I inched my way to the door and outside.

The sun was beginning to set, forming a brilliant gold light above a fog bank. The air was refreshing after the stuffy hall. I was glad to be away from the loud music. I walked around the lodge, the boathouse and onto the wharf. The water lapped softly against the wooden posts and a slight breeze caused the sailboat's rigging to make a delicate twanging noise as it hit against the aluminum mast. I sat down, took off my uncomfortable shoes and put my feet in the water. Then, I heard footsteps. Stefan was walking toward me.

"I saw you leave," he said, a grin spreading across his face. "I'm glad you did."

"You are?" I couldn't believe Stefan was standing so close to me, telling me this.

"Yes, I'd rather talk with you outside than on the dance floor. Don't get me wrong. I like to dance but it's noisy and crowded in there." He paused, and gestured toward the rowboats. "Want to walk the beach?"

"Sure," I replied a bit too quickly.

Then, like a mind reader, he said, "Don't worry. It's a short walk. The chaperones won't miss us yet."

I'd promised myself that I wouldn't break any rules. *But this is different. Stefan isn't just any boy*, I thought as I watched him remove his shoes. He was special and he had come looking for *me*. No, no threats of punishment could keep me from this moment.

We walked off the wharf and onto the cool damp pebbly beach. Impulsively I ran into the frigid water.

"Yikes!" I yelled as I leapt backwards.

Stefan started laughing. "Quite the graceful ballet jump," he said.

I felt heat rising in my face. As we walked on, I hoped I wasn't blushing.

"You must not be from Maine. The Atlantic is always cold. Where *are* you from?"

"Durham, New Hampshire. It's about an hour and a half from Boston. And you?"

"I live in Preston, smack in the middle of Maine." Then, studying my face, he said, "I don't remember you. Were you at the last dance?"

"No, I've only been at Briar Point a week and a half. I won a scholarship for the month of August."

"Congratulations. That's very impressive. I've never met anyone who's won a scholarship to that camp."

Stefan's praise melted away the pain of the previous hour, as I said, "Thanks."

While we walked along the beach, he told me he was

starting the eighth grade in the fall and that he had been coming to Rockhaven Boy Scout Camp for four years. He'd learned to sail the first year at camp and it had become his passion along with camping trips, canoeing, and hiking.

When we turned around at the end of the beach, he asked about my interests. I told him I, too, loved the outdoors, especially hiking and camping, but that my passion was ballet. I told him my desire to become a professional ballerina and travel the world with a ballet company.

We'd returned to the wharf and had put on our shoes when I heard voices nearby. I turned to Stefan and nervously whispered, "What'll we do?"

"Hurry," he said, grabbing my hand. "This way."

We ducked into some shrubs off the path behind the lodge. From there I saw some campers standing outside near the door. The disc jockey was taking his break. We would be missed if we didn't return soon. How would we get inside without being noticed? My heart started to race.

"What now?" I asked, my mind already envisioning Mrs. Weir's angry face.

"We'll have to run and hope no one sees us."

Stefan poked his head out of the shrubs, put his arm around my waist and we darted toward a back door on the other side of the lodge. He opened it and, to my horror, we squeezed inside, right in front of Miss Summers who was getting refreshments from the refrigerator.

Problems

"Jo Price, where on earth have you been?"

I stared at Miss Summers in disbelief. I'd never been caught disobeying. I felt disconnected as if I were watching myself in a movie. "I...I got bored. No one was asking me to dance. So, I left." I clasped my hands to keep them from shaking.

"Go on," she said sternly.

A chill crept through me. My story sounded suspicious. I had no choice but to tell the truth. "Stefan left the dance, too. He saw me on the wharf. We walked on the beach. That's all."

"What were you thinking? No one is allowed to leave the building. This is a very *serious violation* of the rules." She shifted her focus to Stefan. Her face appeared pinched, strained; her eyes assessed him. "What about you, young man? Did you have permission to leave?"

"No," he said, looking at the floor for what seemed an eternity. Miss Summers waited. Finally, Stefan continued, "I wanted some air...less noise. So, I went outside where I saw Jo on the wharf. We walked the beach, just like she said. We did nothing more."

Miss Summers' expression didn't change.

Oh, no, I thought. *I'm in big trouble.* I should have

considered the consequences of leaving the dance. I shouldn't have stayed outside with Stefan. Although I longed to be with him, it hadn't been wise. If Mrs. Weir found out, I could be kicked out of camp and my dancing career could be ruined. I started to tremble.

"Please, Miss Summers," I begged. My voice wavered. My eyes filled with tears. "I shouldn't have left the dance. I apologize. Please don't tell Mrs. Weir."

Miss Summers spoke in a serious but softer tone, "Alright, Mrs. Weir won't know...Both of you will stay in my sight for the rest of the night. Do you understand?" Once we'd agreed, she said, "Jo, you will clean the studios, their bathrooms and dressing rooms at free time until the end of camp. If I *ever* catch you breaking a rule again, you won't go to the next dance."

Relief flowed over my body like a shower. It washed away my fears and left me filled with gratitude. I wouldn't miss the next social dance, leave camp or ruin my dancing career. Mrs. Weir wouldn't even know I'd broken a rule. I hated cleaning toilets, but it was nothing compared to what I could have lost. I thanked Miss Summers with deeply felt appreciation.

She picked up four bottles of Coke, and then left to tell Stefan's chaperones that he'd broken a rule. After she'd gone, I asked Stefan what might happen to him. He said he wasn't sure. He might not be allowed to attend the next social dance. His face looked grim, but then he smiled. Stefan said that, at least, we had the rest of the night together.

When we returned to the dance, girls and boys stood

around the refreshment table talking. Faye and Cece were nowhere in sight. Stefan bought me an orange soda and a brownie. We continued talking. His father was a professor of music at Central Maine University. He had conducted the university orchestra when they'd played Tchaikovsky's score of the *Nutcracker*. A professional ballet company, sponsored by the university's cultural program, had performed. Stefan had seen the ballet several times. He was describing his favorite parts when the disc jockey entered with the rest of the campers.

"Want to dance?" Stefan asked.

"Sure, if we stay near Miss Summers."

"Don't worry. The witch is watching us from her post by the doorway."

"Mrs. Weir is the witch, not Miss Summers. Mrs. Weir would ban me from the last dance or kick me out of camp *for sure*. Miss Summers gave me a break. I hope you'll get one, too."

"I'll do whatever the camp director requires. I've never broken a rule in the four years I've been at camp. So hopefully he'll be lenient."

My entire body tingled when Stefan took me in his arms. As we waltzed, I felt as if I were a feather gliding through the air. Stefan's big brown eyes looked into mine without hesitation. My drooping left eyelid didn't bother him one bit!

We were dancing our third dance when I felt a tap on my shoulder. Startled, I turned around. Cece was there. "I'm cutting in," she informed me.

Devastated, like Cinderella after the ball, I returned to the side of the room. *Faye's right,* I thought. *Cece's different around boys.* She doesn't care if she hurts me as long as she dances with Stefan.

Ladies' choice was announced next. I tried to compose myself enough to ask Stefan to dance. I wasn't fast enough. Cece asked first.

As I watched her move her body seductively against his, I wanted to yank her away and yell, "Leave him alone! He's mine! You have plenty of boyfriends!" My body tensed. Anger, hot as fire, burned in my stomach. I clenched my teeth. I tried deep breathing. Nothing helped.

After a while a tall lanky boy, who'd danced with Cece earlier, cut in. Maybe it was my imagination, but Stefan looked relieved. Instead of returning to me, he talked with a friend at the refreshment table.

Maybe I'm wrong. Maybe Stefan preferred Cece. Had he already forgotten me? Several dances later, however, he approached me, took my hand and guided me onto the dance floor. As we danced, the floating sensation returned. It swept over me like a cloud gliding effortlessly over the earth. I rested my head against his shoulder, closed my eyes. Bliss filled me. The room disappeared. Stefan and I danced as one, alone. Nothing existed but the movement and warmth of his body against mine. We danced every dance for the rest of the night. I'd never felt *such joy!* During the last dance, I vowed to remember this night forever.

Afterwards, Stefan gently squeezed me closer and

said, "Thanks for a great night. Stay out of trouble. You don't want to miss the next dance. There's a cookout before it. Maybe I can get permission to use the sailboat."

"Don't worry. I wouldn't miss it for the world. But you'd better behave." I gave him a funny smirk. "Otherwise *you* won't be at the dance!"

I met up with Faye while heading to the bus. She told me Cece was hopping mad with me for dancing with Stefan. I hadn't seen Faye or Cece during the last half of the dance but obviously they'd spoken.

"What right does Cece have being mad? Stefan chose to dance with me."

"You'll be her target anyway. I told you. She's different around boys."

From the bus, we watched Cece write something on a piece of paper and hand it to the tall, lanky red-head. Faye guessed that she'd given him Briar Point's phone number. When Cece marched past, Faye asked her. She nodded and, without glancing at me, headed to the back of the bus. Sadness colored Faye's face. "She'll ignore you, Jo," Faye said, "wait and see."

How would I handle this? Though upset, I felt oddly honored. I had a boyfriend and Cece was *jealous*. I'd never had anyone *jealous of me*.

As the bus moved toward camp, I closed my eyes. The problem could wait. I wanted to soak up the pleasure of the evening: Stefan's hand warm against my back as we glided around the dance floor, the kind look in his eyes. My memories stopped abruptly when the bus pulled up at the main house. Outside the building, I waited.

"Cece," I said as she approached, "I just want to talk with you." She pierced me with a devilish expression and turned away.

৵৽৹

Three days later, Cece was still avoiding me. Faye urged her to discuss the situation with me, but she refused. I hated being treated like I was invisible; I missed the old fun-loving Cece.

No one knew that I'd left the dance and had been given a punishment. I simply told Faye that Miss Summers had given me a job cleaning the studios. Thus, no one, especially Cece, would know my secret.

I thought about Stefan constantly except during dance classes when I concentrated on learning the choreography for my ballet and jazz classes. Often, I wondered what he was doing and daydreamed of dancing with him. I also daydreamed about Mr. Capp but not as often. During his class, however, I kept hoping he would touch me again.

That day, after lunch, I felt strange. My stomach and lower back ached. While sweeping the Stonegate dressing room, I realized I'd started to menstruate. I was *horrified, unprepared.* Everyone else's periods had begun. I'd pretended mine had, too. So, I couldn't ask anyone for help. What would I do? I held my stomach as the pain increased.

Just then, the studio door opened and shut. I heard a familiar popular song being played. Clutching the broom, I entered the studio. Miss Summers turned around. "Jo, are you OK? You look pale," she said.

I told her I didn't feel well. I moved closer and whispered that my first period had come. Mom hadn't spoken with me about menstruating. I'd only seen a short movie about it in gym class. I had no clue what to do. I felt pathetically naïve.

To my surprise, Miss Summers smiled pleasantly

and exclaimed, "That's wonderful! Come here. I have everything you need."

Why was starting my period wonderful? I was sore and achy. But I felt comforted, as Miss Summers wrapped an arm around me. She led me to the bathroom where she explained what to do. I thanked her repeatedly, but my words seemed inadequate. *It's odd how things work out,* I thought. If Miss Summers hadn't given me a punishment for leaving the dance, my period might have come when she wasn't around to help.

Making Up

The following day, near the end of class, Miss Summers assigned girls to choreograph dances to share at our last class, a bit less than two weeks away. When she grouped Faye, Cece and me, Cece grimaced. "I can't work with Jo. We're not friends now," she announced.

Her words echoed around the studio. Everyone stared at me. No one spoke. My face burned hot. Immediately, the loss of Laura's friendship to Leslie Louise reared its ugly head like a recurring nightmare.

"I see," Miss Summers said. After a brief pause, she continued, "Sooner or later, Cece, you'll have to work with people you dislike. So, I'm not changing your group." Why didn't Miss Summers separate us? How could we work together? Cece wasn't talking with me. Addressing the class, Miss Summers said, "OK. You're to choreograph a dance with your group. Find music you like or select a record of mine. The day after tomorrow, your group will show the class what you've choreographed so far. Go have some fun."

Fun, she must be kidding, I thought.

Faye picked out one of Miss Summers's records and we left the studio. Faye gave me a pained look as we headed to sports with Cece.

Then, shocking myself, I blurted out, "This is *stupid*,

Cece. I did *nothing wrong*."

"You stole Stefan from me," she hissed.

"He wasn't yours."

"*Yes he was!* You knew I adored him. You messed up my plans." She glared at me.

Silence followed. Finally, Faye asked Cece, "What about the red-head you danced with for most of the night?"

"Oh, Alex, he's OK, I guess, but he's not that interested in me. Alex just wanted someone to dance with. Besides he's not handsome like Stefan."

"So what? Walter isn't handsome but he's nice. If Alex isn't interested in you, why'd he want Briar Point's phone number?"

"Who knows? Your guess is as good as mine."

We separated at the rec hall, where I found my tennis partner. Afterwards, I left for Stonegate to clean the studio, grateful to miss seeing Cece or Faye.

Then, on my way to dinner, Cece approached me, smiling hugely. "Let's make up," she said, in an animated voice.

"*What!*" I exclaimed. Why was she so cheerful? What had caused her sudden change of heart?

"Let's make up," she repeated.

She wasn't getting off that easily. "You embarrassed me in front of the *whole class*. How do you think I felt?"

"I'm sorry," she said, a bit too quickly.

"*Sorry!* Is that all you can say? You accused me of *stealing* your boyfriend. I *didn't*."

"I know. You didn't. I get possessive around boys. I was being childish."

"*Yes, you were!*"

"I'm truly sorry I hurt you. Please forgive me. Can we make up?"

"OK," I said, still reluctant and perplexed. "But, let's be clear. Stefan and I will be together at the next social. So, *don't interfere.*"

"I won't, promise. Stefan never was my type anyway. I tried relating to him, but we had little in common," she stated. "I'm *totally in love* with Alex now. After dinner, let's work on the dance and miss the evening event. Faye has set up her room so that we have a small dance space."

She wasn't surprised that we'd reconciled when we arrived. Maybe she'd convinced Cece to apologize. Or she knew something. I would find out.

Faye put the record on her small portable record player and began choreographing. She positioned me in front of Cece and herself, on my knees with my head down. Their heads also hung down, hands at hips. On the musical introduction, I stood up and placed my hands like theirs. Together we lifted our heads. As the lyrics began, we did a jazz square, two <u>step-ball-changes</u> and twirled to the right. Faye's steps fit the music perfectly.

During a bathroom break, I asked Faye about Cece's change of heart. Faye explained, "Mrs. Weir had a phone call from Alex's Rock Haven camp counselor. He asked permission for Alex to meet Cece this Friday at the horse farm to watch her ride Dylan. The camp counselor will chaperone. So, Mrs. Weir agreed. She told Cece at free time today. Naturally, she is delighted."

"So, she's not interested in Stefan anymore?"

"Nope."

It made sense. Cece had her serious boyfriend. So, it was easy for her to apologize. Faye was right when she'd described Cece as boy-crazy!

When she returned, Faye choreographed more of the dance, adding some of our suggestions. Tomorrow, we would skip the evening event again to work on the choreography.

৩৯৯৫

The next morning, I awoke thinking about ballet class. Mr. Capp had started teaching us the choreography to a piece by Bizet for the final show. I'd struggled to remember the dance, unlike my peers. In addition, the new step, a <u>sissonne</u> <u>ouverte</u> <u>a</u> <u>la</u> <u>seconde</u>, posed a challenge. It was difficult keeping my right leg up to the side while landing on my left leg in a plié. Today, would my sissonne improve? Would I remember the dance sequence? I tossed the blankets off and dressed, determined to succeed.

Before ballet class, several girls were marking the dance. I joined them, grateful they'd remembered it. During class, however, discouragement set in. Although my sissonne was better, I chided myself for relying on my classmates to remember the choreography.

After class, I spoke with Mr. Capp about my concerns. He appeared undisturbed. "Of all the dancers in this class, you have made the most progress." Did he really mean this? I felt my face flush at his compliment. "Don't worry about remembering the choreography. It comes with repetition. Now, hurry and go to arts and crafts or Mrs. Schneider will think you're absent."

I left the studio feeling blissfully lighthearted, like a bird drifting effortlessly on a breeze.

The Emergency

The next day during sports, Faye asked me, "When you clean the carriage house studio, would you tell Julia I won't be practicing today?"

"Sure. No problem."

"Too bad I have to miss my favorite tutor!" she added, faking a frown. We grinned as we put our tennis rackets back.

On the way to the carriage house, massive rain clouds darkened the sky. The wind tossed pine needles about, a flurry of whirling green shapes. Huge raindrops fell. I ran to the door and yanked it open. There, on the floor by the record player, lay Julia, motionless.

"Julia," I shrieked, running to her. "Julia, wake up!" Was she dead? A chill ran through me. I leaned down, touched her arm, and shook her gently. She didn't move. Her chest rose slightly. Her eyelids fluttered but didn't open. What should I do? Oh...Mr. Capp. Yelling his name, I bounded outside, up the stairs. I pounded on his door, tried the doorknob. It was locked.

Back in the studio, Julia hadn't moved. I left her and raced toward the main house for help. The rain, heavy now, pelted my body. In the distance, I saw Mr. Capp heading toward me. I ran to him, screaming, "Julia's on the studio floor!" Trying to catch my breath, I gasped, "She's not moving."

"What happened?"

"I don't know. I found her that way."

"Is she breathing?"

"Barely."

"OK. I'll call an ambulance. Go get Mrs. Weir." He sprinted toward the carriage house.

Although I ran as fast as I could, I felt like I was in slow motion. Breathing hard, my side aching, I found Mrs. Weir's office empty. I dashed into the kitchen where she was talking with the cook. "Mrs. Weir," I yelled, straining to breath. "It's Julia. She's collapsed. She's hardly breathing. Mr. Capp is calling an ambulance. He needs you at the carriage house."

Her mouth dropped open. Her face paled. "Not Julia!" she moaned. "Oh, my God."

Grabbing my arm, she pulled me to her office. There, she opened a notebook, dialed the telephone and waited, tapping her fingers on the table.

"Hello, Mr. Carmichael, this is Mrs. Weir. Julia collapsed in the studio." She paused to listen, and then said, "No, we don't know what happened. We're waiting for the ambulance. I'll call when she gets to the hospital. OK. Bye." Turning to me, she said, "Mr. Weir is away on business. So, we've got to find Miss Summers." She motioned for me to follow her as she ran to Stonegate. Miss Summers wasn't there. We dashed to Mrs. Weir's car. She pulled out of the parking spot nearly bashing into the portico. Tires screeched as Mrs.

Weir sped to the carriage house. In the distance, I could hear the mournful wail of the ambulance.

When we arrived, the ambulance driver and his assistant had already strapped Julia's frail ghost-like body to a stretcher. Her eyes remained closed. I wondered if she was still breathing.

Mrs. Weir rushed to her, crying, "Julia, can you hear me? Julia!" Getting no response, Mrs. Weir asked the ambulance driver, "What's wrong with her?"

"I don't know. Does she have any history of seizures, diabetes or heart problems?"

"None."

"We've got to get her to the hospital, out of the rain," he stated as he and his assistant quickly slid the stretcher in the ambulance. Mr. Capp climbed up to sit beside Julia.

Mrs. Weir looked panicky. "Jo," she ordered. "Go find Miss Summers. Tell her Mr. Capp and I have gone to the hospital. She's in charge until I return." Mrs. Weir fled to her car, following the ambulance out the back road.

Hot tears and cold rain streamed down my face as I headed toward the main house again. Dark clouds, like fear, hovered over me. Julia, only a few years older than me, couldn't die. Could she? I didn't like her very much, but I silently prayed. *Please, God, don't let Julia die. Please.*

At Miss Summers's cabin, I told her about Julia and relayed Mrs. Weir's message. We walked in silence to the main house. I immediately went to Faye's room. Cece was with her. They looked relieved as both of them rushed to me.

Faye spoke first. "Oh, Jo, thank goodness you're OK. We were *so* worried. We heard the ambulance going toward the carriage house."

"What happened?" asked Cece.

"Julia was on the floor when I went in to clean the carriage house. I was in shock. I thought she was dead. The ambulance driver doesn't know what's wrong with her. Mrs. Weir and Mr. Capp are at the hospital with her now." Faye and Cece looked terrified. Neither spoke. I continued, spewing out more details in an attempt to make sense of the crisis. "Julia was hardly breathing when I first saw her."

"What did you do?" Concern spread across Faye's face taking the color out of it.

"I shouted her name, shook her. When she didn't move, I feared she would *die right in front of me*."

"Oh, no," exclaimed Cece.

"It was horrible to think Julia might die before I could get help. Luckily, I found Mr. Capp on my way to the main house. He rushed off to call the ambulance while I found Mrs. Weir. Together we reached the carriage house just as Julia was being put into the ambulance. She looked the same...*nearly dead*." I began crying hysterically, shaking uncontrollably.

Faye wrapped a bath towel tightly around me. Speaking calmly, she said, "Take a deep breath, Jo. You're drenched and shivering." Putting her arm around my shoulder, she said, "Come on, Cece and I will walk you to your room so you can change clothes and rest before dinner."

Rehearsing

Back in my room, I changed clothes and, exhausted, flopped on my bed. An uneasy silence filled the room. Beside me, Julia's bed waited impatiently, as if it were reflecting my mood. When would I hear if Julia was alive? Footsteps and voices broke the silence as girls went to dinner. Instead of joining them, I rolled over and fell asleep.

Later, I awoke to knocking at my door. I looked at my clock. It was midnight. Mrs. Weir entered my room. Dark circles had formed under her eyes, her hair askew. I'd never seen her so unkempt. "Sorry to wake you. Julia's in stable condition. She's going to be fine. The doctors are doing tests. We'll know more soon."

"Thank goodness," I said.

"Thank you for helping to save her life."

I didn't know what to say. Had I really helped save her life? The thought pierced me. Tears flooded my eyes.

Mrs. Weir didn't notice my teary eyes, or she pretended not to. "Do you want anything to eat before you go back to sleep?"

"No thanks."

"OK, sleep well," she said, as she quietly closed the door.

❦

At breakfast Mrs. Weir announced that Julia was in fair condition at Central Maine Regional Hospital. She would be there a week. The girls at my table stared at one another. Finally, one of them asked Mrs. Weir what we all wanted to know. "Will she be able to dance in the final show?"

"I don't know. She's extremely weak. We'll have to wait and see. In the meantime, an understudy will be chosen."

There was a buzz in the room as girls speculated on who would be Julia's understudy. Leaving the dining hall, I overheard Norma, one of the girls at my table, speaking with Mr. Capp. "I've already memorized Julia's parts. So, I'll make the perfect understudy. What do you think?"

"We'll see, Norma." He sighed deeply. "This is not an appropriate time to discuss Julia's replacement." He turned his back on her and walked out of the dining hall.

What nerve! Julia's in grave danger. Meanwhile, Norma's scheming, like a cat about to pounce on its prey, to get Julia's part in the ballet. I vowed I'd never act like Norma.

❦

At jazz class, we performed our dance before the others

so that Miss Summers could see what we'd choreo-graphed so far. She suggested our group change some steps and travel around our imaginary stage instead of dancing mostly in one place.

Faye looked downcast. She said nothing on the way to sports. At our practice time during evening events, Faye was close to tears. "Miss Summers *hates* my cho-reography."

"That's not true," insisted Cece. "She's just giving us constructive criticism to make our dance better."

Faye, who was always upbeat, didn't comment. I put my arm around her and said, "You'll make the changes easily. You've got the awesome talent to create dances. Not everyone has that."

"Miss. Summers doesn't think so," argued Faye.

"Oh, come on, Faye, that's not true. *For heaven's sake*, don't let us down now," Cece said. "You know *we* can't choreograph."

"She's right," I chimed in. "Our dance is doomed without you. Why don't we use the Stonegate studio at free time? You can choreograph with Cece and teach me my part once I've cleaned."

Reluctantly, Faye agreed, and, after sports, she got the record from her room, put it on the record player, and began moving to the music. From the bathroom, I heard her explaining moves to Cece.

Once I finished cleaning, I joined them and watched as they performed the new choreography. Their move-ments swept from one side of the room to the other, filling the space well. After Faye had taught me my part, and we'd finished rehearsing, she looked at us confidently and said, "This dance is a hundred percent better. Now, I'm actually glad Miss. Summers didn't like the old version."

❦

The next day after class, Mr. Capp approached me, smiling broadly. "I'd like you to learn Daphne's part in the polka piece. She's Julia's understudy. Are you interested?" Shocked, I wondered if I'd heard him correctly. Was I really capable of dancing with the level-3 dancers? Could I keep up with them? I'd heard the advanced dancers discussing the piece. It was the "Bartered Bride Polka," by the composer Smetana. I knew it was difficult, extremely fast and there wasn't much time to learn it. Noticing my anxiety, Mr. Capp added, "Of course I'll rehearse with you individually before you practice with the other girls."

Me...practicing alone with Mr. Capp! I couldn't believe it!

"Yes. That sounds wonderful...thank you *so much*."

"Good. We'll start tomorrow. I've arranged for you to miss sports for the next two days so I can teach you the choreography. Then you'll join the level-3 class, which is during your arts and crafts class. I've spoken with Mrs. Schneider and she understands that you won't be there."

"Great!" I said.

I left the studio elated. I couldn't wait to see Faye's

expression when I told her I'd be practicing the polka piece *alone with Mr. Capp!*

❧

Mr. Capp had finished rehearsing Julia's part with Daphne when I arrived the next afternoon. I didn't know her well. But she greeted me pleasantly and offered to help me if I needed it. Daphne had been chosen over Norma, which pleased me.

After she left, Mr. Capp and I listened to the music for the polka piece. The footwork proved challenging. Though I knew the steps, doing them at the fast tempo seemed almost impossible. I practiced them repeatedly without improvement. Exhausted, close to tears, I sank to the floor. I'd failed Mr. Capp. He sat down beside me and took my hands. I felt the same delightful tingle I had a few weeks earlier. When I looked into his kind face, I choked up. "Maybe you should pick someone else," I managed.

"Don't give up on yourself so fast. You can't expect to master this in one day." He paused. "The more advanced level-3 girls will end the dance and I know you can handle the beginning and middle sections. So, let's stop now. We'll rehearse again tomorrow, and then you'll join the others. Don't worry. You'll master the dance." He patted my shoulder before getting up. I savored his touch as I headed to the main house.

❧

Two days later, I nervously watched the level-3 dancers enter the studio, but when Daphne smiled at me, I relaxed. Mr. Capp instructed me to follow her as she danced her old part. We rehearsed it several times. Other dancers showed me where to move on the imaginary stage, which had been taped down on the studio floor, and practiced the fast part with me. Joy swept through me, like sunlight streaming through the studio windows. For the first time, I felt accepted by the level-3 dancers!

We were almost finished rehearsing when Mrs. Weir entered the studio. Everyone stopped dancing. She had never interrupted before. With a sad face, she stared at us. "I'm sorry to tell you that Julia won't be returning to camp. Her doctors say she's been starving herself and that she's not strong enough to dance. Julia will go home soon."

Now I understood why Julia had eaten so little and exercised so much. Although I felt sad about her situation, I was simultaneously overjoyed. Daphne and I would dance our new parts! My heart beat rapidly. I'd be performing with the advanced dancers, most of them moving toward professional ballet careers. Maybe Mr. Capp thought I, too, had talent!

The Last Social Dance

Cece forced her way into my room unannounced. "Look, Jo, another letter from Alex! He sent pictures; that's me on Dylan." The last dance was two days away. Alex was all she talked about.

I'd become as obsessed with Stefan. What was he doing? Did he think of me? In my daydreams, he'd hold my hands or wrap his arms around me. He'd lean close. I'd close my eyes and he'd kiss me, long and tender.

Now, Cece was showing me a photograph she'd taken of Alex. "Did you know that he and Walter are best friends? We'll be at the cookout with Faye and him before the dance. Want to join us?"

"Sure. That'd be fun," I said.

She took her pictures, headed to the door, and said, "I *must* show Faye these before quiet time. See ya."

৶৯৹৶

The night before the social, Faye curled my hair on wire-brush rollers. I looked like an alien insect with a huge head. Mom would be horrified. I felt like a happy rebel when I left for bed. But, by midnight, the curlers had dug into my skull. I yanked them out, tossed them violently on the floor, swearing that I'd never sleep with those cruel curlers ever again. Finally, I fell asleep.

In the morning, my slightly curly hair bounced around my face. I hated the killer curlers littering the floor but I loved my new look. I couldn't wait for Stefan to see my curls!

Later that day, we found seats on the bus, cramming our dresses, makeup bags and other paraphernalia on our laps. We, unrealistically, hoped to keep our dresses wrinkle free. At the boys' camp, we left our gear in the clubhouse. Mr. Harkman, the camp director we'd met before, entered. He welcomed us again to the Rockhaven Boy Scout Camp, where they were celebrating their twentieth anniversary with special events, a cookout and the social dance. After explaining the schedule, he directed us outside to the rowboat relay race. Two rowboats rested on the water's edge, one for the bluebird team, the other for the eagle team. Each team had half their boys on the beach while the other half waited on a platform several hundred yards out on the water.

Where was Stefan? I didn't see him anywhere. Was he on the platform? I couldn't see that far. Had he been banned for breaking the rules? My energy plummeted like a rock hitting the ground.

A whistle blew. A boy from each team jumped into a rowboat. They pushed their oars furiously, tossing water up, trying to reach the platform first. There, team members exchanged places, rowing back to shore as fast as possible. Everyone was screaming for their favorite team. The bluebird team was ahead. Near the end of the race, I finally saw Stefan! Relief swept through me. He was plowing his rowboat, for the eagle team, at tremendous speed toward the shore. But he was outraced. After the relay, he gave me a huge smile. "You can't win 'em all," he said, as though talking to himself. Then, looking at me, he said, "I'm glad you stayed out of trouble and came."

"I wouldn't miss this for *anything*."

He took my hand. "Come on. Let's play badminton."

After playing several rounds, we joined Faye, Walter, Cece, and Alex for hamburgers and hot dogs at the cookout. Then Faye, Cece, and I headed to the clubhouse, which had been set up for the Briar Point Ballet Campers to change for the dance.

Once everyone had changed, we entered the lodge where giant paper butterflies and ladybugs, decorated in a variety of brilliant colors, hung from the ceiling along with a banner that read: *Congratulations, Rockhaven, Celebrating Twenty Years of Boy Scouting.* A disc jockey, standing under the banner, started the evening with a ladies' choice dance. Glowing, I asked Stefan for the dance. I led him onto the floor as a beautiful slow melody started. In his arms, I felt delightful sensations, even better than those in my daydreams! We danced to the next song, and then the next until we'd danced *every dance.* Suddenly I realized that Stefan didn't care if I was pretty or popular. He just liked me!

After a few more dances, Stefan motioned for me to follow him. Keeping his eyes on Miss Summers, who was chaperoning again, he succeeded in guiding us unnoticed into the kitchen. We drank orange sodas as we admired the camp's anniversary cake. Then, surprising me, Stefan leaned down, softly kissing my lips. A rush of pleasant sensations pulsed through me. We were about to kiss again when we heard Miss Summers's voice and footsteps approaching the kitchen. She'd warned me to stay within her sight during the dance. *Oh, no, not again*, I thought. If she finds me here, I'll be punished *again*! She'll tell Mrs. Weir and I'll be banned from the final dance performance *for sure. Why had I been so careless?*

I looked around the room. The pantry, near us, was dark and long. I motioned to Stefan. We slipped into its back corner, sliding onto the floor behind some large food containers. Next, I heard drawers opening, then closing and Mr. Harkman's voice, "I have the candles but I can't find any matches."

"They must be here. I'll look in the pantry," said Miss Summers.

My body went cold. I held my breath. My heart pounded in my ears.

"Never mind," replied Mr. Harkman. "I found them."

Relieved, then horrified, I saw Miss Summers walk into the pantry with the cake, turn to a counter and begin lighting the candles. Our hiding place grew brighter and brighter. If she turned slightly to her left, she'd see us.

Thankfully, she returned to the kitchen, moments later, with the candle-lit cake. Suddenly darkness surrounded us, except for the dim glow from the candles. After Miss Summers took the cake to the refreshment table, Stefan and I ran quickly out to join the others. I cringed as Miss Summers approached Stefan and me. Although I didn't think she'd seen us, I started to apologize, "I know I shouldn't have..."

Interrupting me, she exclaimed, "Oh, no, you should have cake, Jo!" She smiled at us. "You both should celebrate Rockhaven's twentieth anniversary. Don't you think so?"

Stunned, Stefan took a moment to recover, "Sure...sure we should."

"Well, go get some cake before it's all gone," she instructed, and then left.

Stefan and I burst out laughing when Miss Summers was far enough away.

The lights dimmed when the disc jockey announced the last dance. Above me, the decorations looked magical in the low light. The butterflies and ladybugs appeared to flit around us spreading a golden glitter. Slow sensuous music started. Stefan held me tight. My head on his shoulder, we swayed to the melody. Nothing mattered but the movement of our bodies, gliding together. If only this moment would last!

With the decorations being removed and the bright lights on, the lodge returned to its normal dull self. It was time to leave. Stefan stood beside me in the bus line. He handed me a paper with his address on it. As I boarded the bus, he said, "See you next summer."

Before I could reply, Miss Summers closed the door. I tried, without luck, to push her aside, desperate to tell Stefan that I wouldn't be back. Feeling depleted, I passed Faye and Cece, who'd found seats together. Alone at the end of the bus, I watched Stefan grow smaller as the bus moved away. Finally, only the camp lights sparkled across the cove. I wouldn't see Stefan again. I clutched the paper he'd given me tightly in my hand. Tears dropped slowly. What a cruel trick of fate, finding a boyfriend hundreds of miles away. I'd be home soon, like it or not. Now, however, if I wasn't asked to dance at the Oyster River Junior High social dances, I wouldn't care. I wiped my eyes, smiled and silently thanked Stefan.

Show Preparations

"Let the music get inside you, Jo," suggested Miss Summers. "Listen to the rhythm. It goes da, de-da, da, da, de-da, de-da, da, da. The counts are one, and two, three, four, and five, and six, seven, eight. It's tricky. Follow me, slowly."

It was the next day. We were practicing the Duke Ellington dance, our group number, for the final performance. Everyone, except me, had mastered the choreography. I sensed my classmates' impatience while Miss Summers demonstrated the last thirty-two counts repeatedly. Quick ballet steps, especially new ones, always challenged me, but quick jazz steps, like a foreign language, posed an even greater challenge. Although I'd mastered the first part of the dance, I knew I could ruin the ending if I didn't learn it *and soon*. I sighed.

"Don't worry. Have fun. If you're enjoying the dance, the audience will, too. They won't even know you've made a mistake." Miss Summers's positive attitude always reminded me to be less serious; if I didn't learn the last counts, it wouldn't be the end of the world.

I was about to try again when I heard the studio door creak open, then bang shut. Mrs. Weir stumbled in carrying two huge boxes of costumes. Everyone forgot the rules and swarmed around her, talking and shoving.

"Girls, quiet down," demanded Mrs. Weir. "I can't hear myself think." She set the boxes down and began handing out the costumes, which were more elegant than I'd imagined. Black sleeveless leotards with turquoise skirts, were edged in sequins and a small sequined hat featured a feather attached to its front.

I felt uncomfortable in the dressing room with half-naked girls casually changing. I turned around to don my costume, embarrassed about my developing breasts. The costume, soft and silky, fit perfectly. Peering in the studio mirror, I forgot my embarrassment. I looked beautiful, and felt sexy. If only Stefan could see me now! Just then, Faye and several other girls complimented me. I beamed, proud of my new figure.

After sports, I returned to my room to find a letter from my parents on Julia's abandoned bed. Depression suddenly overtook me. Acid built up in my stomach. I stared at the envelope. Memories returned. Like water overflowing a dam, I couldn't hold back feelings of humiliation, fear, and self-pity. I'd be leaving camp, my dance teachers, friends, and Stefan. A lump formed in my throat. I couldn't swallow. I looked away from the letter. I have to stop thinking like this, I told myself. I'm getting too upset. Things change. Durham would be the same. I wouldn't. Besides, I reminded myself, at home I had my ballet friends and Mrs. Evans's classes. I was old enough now to approach my parents about traveling to the Boston Ballet School by bus on Saturdays. I needed to maintain the strength and techniques I'd learned from camp to continue my ballet career.

Feeling a bit better, I opened the letter. My parents were coming *two days before the performance*! They *already* had motel reservations in Briar Cove and had decided to combine seeing the performance and taking me home with a sketching trip for Dad, who spent summer vacations drawing and painting landscapes. They planned to stop by briefly the day before the show. Why were they doing this? Everyone's parents had been notified to come *only* the day of the performance and, afterward, take their daughters home. Hadn't they read the letter? Didn't they know they'd embarrass me? Nobody else's parents would be visiting. I desperately needed time with my friends, *not my parents*. In utter frustration, I beat my pillow to a pulp. Exhausted, I flung myself on top of it. I had to stop them. I would beg Mrs. Weir to let me use the phone.

I went downstairs to her office. Mrs. Weir was shuffling through some papers at her desk when I poked my head through the doorway.

"Sorry to bother you, Mrs. Weir," I began. "May I please use the phone to call my parents? They didn't get the notice about coming only on the day of the performance and they wrote me that they plan to come early."

"Oh, for heaven's sakes! I thought, for sure, that we'd notified everyone's parents. I'm sorry. Of course you can use the phone."

I thanked her profusely and rushed off. My hands shook as I dialed the number. What if my parents had already left for Briar Cove? I wondered. After three rings, Mom answered. I asked her if she'd received the notice not to come until the last day. She had received it, but my parents thought a brief visit before then would be OK. *No,* I insisted. *It would not be OK.* Mom must have heard my sharp tone of voice. She said they would be in the area, so that Dad could sketch, but they wouldn't come until the performance.

After I hung up, I slumped back against the chair, pleased that I'd avoided a huge disaster. My parents wouldn't be embarrassing me or wrecking the last days with my friends.

❦

It started raining on the way to dress rehearsal in a nearby gymnasium. I peered out the bus window at a dark slate-gray sky, similar to the day I'd come to camp. Then, I'd been tearful, lonely and afraid. Now, I didn't want to leave. Shielding our costumes from the rain, we rushed into the building. It felt like a steam bath as we entered a large locker room that smelled of dirty gym clothes. I tugged at my tights, which stuck defiantly to my legs, and I yanked on my ballet costume.

Mr. Capp placed tape on the stage floor, like the choreographers and teachers at the Boston Ballet had done during final rehearsal for the "Stars and Stripes" solo. "Girls, notice your relationship to these pieces of tape as you dance," he said, pointing to their placement on the floor. "Remember to keep your lines straight by following the dancer in the front."

When the music started, I had to travel, which

meant, in this case, that I had to enlarge my steps and move faster to dance across the length of the stage. As instructed, I noted my place in relationship to the tape and I tried my best to keep behind the line leader. By the end of my part, I was sweating profusely from making my steps big enough.

After the first run-through, Mr. Capp instructed the lighting director to put pink and purple spotlights on us. Our long white skirts instantly became a rosy lavender, casting beautiful maroon shadows. The extra lights added to the already unbearable heat. During the second run-through, rain pounded the gym roof so loudly that I hardly heard the music.

After the ballet number, I rushed to the locker room. Faye and Cece helped me change into my jazz costume. There was no time to be embarrassed. The Duke Ellington piece followed the dance being rehearsed. My heart was pounding as hard as the rain smashing against the locker room windows.

Dressed, and in the wings, I tried to calm myself. We were on stage before I'd caught my breath. There, Miss Summers positioned us on the stage and started the music. The Duke Ellington piece was going well. We weren't yet to the middle of the dance when the lights suddenly went out. In totally darkness, a loud clap of thunder pierced the silence. Several girls screamed; no one moved. No one spoke. I only heard Mr. Capp's muffled voice as he spoke with the stage crew. A thin column of light danced weirdly about. It threw odd-shaped shadows on the stage as Mr. Capp approached carrying a flashlight. "Don't panic. Stay where you are. Let's not be melodramatic. It's only a passing storm. We'll wait for the power to return."

Within a few minutes, Miss Summers and Mrs. Weir arrived with their flashlights and the stage lost its eerie quality. Finally, after half an hour or more, Mr. Capp explained the situation. "The electricity may not come on for several hours. So, we'll be leaving soon. The day after tomorrow, we'll arrive, a few minutes before the performance, so the jazz dancers can rehearse their piece again. Take off your costumes, get dressed, and then line up at the gym door."

On the bus ride back, Mrs. Weir attempted to reassure us. She stated an old performance adage: the worse the rehearsal; the better the show. I prayed she was right.

The Last Day

I'd been screaming at my parents when the morning bell woke me. Why had I been so angry? I stretched, like a sleepy cat, got up and dressed, but I kept thinking about the dream until it slowly returned. My parents' plans had changed. They would be coming early. *Oh, thank goodness*, I thought. It was only a dream.

At breakfast, I sat at Cece and Faye's table, which was against the rules, but I didn't care. We chatted about the upcoming performance as we gobbled down the special buttermilk pancakes with maple syrup.

Upstairs, I was changing into my leotard and tights when I heard a loud knock on my door. *Oh, no, my dream has come true,* I realized. *My parents are here!* They were supposed to meet me after the performance. Why were they here? I almost yelled for them to *go away.* "One minute," I replied instead, purposefully taking as long as I could before opening the door.

Allison stood there. "*Surprise!*" she yelled.

"Wow, Allison!" I shrieked, hugging her tightly. "What...what's?"

She completed my question, "What's going on? I'm spending the day with you!"

"You are?!"

"*Yes!* Mrs. Weir called Mrs. Evans and asked if she

could bring a friend of yours to visit for the day. When Mrs. Weir heard that I'd danced in the Boston Ballet's Summer Program, she suggested I take classes with you. Mrs. Weir said she'd planned this as a surprise because you helped to save Julia. What did she mean?"

"It's a long story. I'll tell you later. Where's Mrs. Evans?"

"She's waiting in the lounge."

On the way downstairs, we talked about Allison's summer. Her experience had been amazing. Allison had met such high standards of performance and ballet technique that the director of the summer program had offered her a full scholarship for next summer. Naturally, she'd accepted the offer immediately. Allison had made loads of friends and, of course, raved about the boys she'd met in partnering classes. She'd just returned home a week ago.

"Did we surprise you?" asked Mrs. Evans, as we entered the lounge. She grinned from ear to ear, just like the Cheshire Cat from *Alice in Wonderland*.

"For sure!" I squealed in delight and flew into her arms.

We heard Mrs. Weir approaching, her high heels clicking loudly on the wooden floor. She extended her hand to Mrs. Evans. "It's lovely to meet you. Jo's an outstanding young lady. It's been a real pleasure having her at camp."

Turning her attention to Allison, she continued, "I'm so happy you could join us. I hope you'll enjoy taking classes with Jo today." Then, to my total shock, she asked Mrs. Evans if Allison could spend the night, and, if so, she could sleep in Julia's old bed.

Spend the night! I thought. *Wow.* I stared at Mrs. Weir in disbelief. She gave me a huge grin and a wink. I'd never felt close to Mrs. Weir but, suddenly, I wanted to hug her.

It was no problem for Allison to stay. Mrs. Evans would cancel the reservations she'd made at a local inn and spend the night with her brother who lived an hour away. After breakfast, she would pick up Allison, and then they would go to the performance together.

I thanked Mrs. Weir and, once we'd taken Allison's suitcase from Mrs. Evans's car and watched her leave, we raced upstairs where Allison changed into her dance clothes. Then we dashed to the Carriage House.

Mr. Capp gave me a quizzical look when he saw Allison with me. I introduced them and explained that Mrs. Weir was letting her be my guest. During the class, Mr. Capp, upon recognizing Allison's talent, had her demonstrate a fouetté turn that we'd all been struggling to master. We watched as she extended her right leg to the front, whipped it around to her side and bent in her knee. By repeating this sequence, she spun around like a toy top. I counted eight beautifully executed turns before she stopped. Although everyone applauded, I could almost hear the other dancers' thoughts as if they'd spoken them aloud. What right did Allison have to show off her technique when she hadn't even been a camper? I didn't care what they thought. Besides, I knew Allison wouldn't let their jealousy bother her.

Following the level-3 class, on our way to the dining hall, we met up with Faye and Cece. Both girls recalled Allison from stories I'd told and they easily struck up a conversation with her as if she'd always been with us.

Finished with lunch, the four of us gathered in my room. No one cared about breaking the quiet-time rule. We weren't losing our last opportunity to be together. Besides, we were dying to see Allison's professional photographs that she'd had taken during the Boston Ballet's Summer Program. We teased her relentlessly when we saw Allison with her male partner. Although she enjoyed partnering, Allison confessed that it hadn't been easy, especially when her partner was learning to lift her. In the process, Allison's ribs had been badly bruised. None-the-less, she said it had been worth it!

Later, we headed to Stonegate where Miss Summers greeted Allison in her usual warm, bubbly fashion and encouraged her to join us. Even though, like me, Allison hadn't studied jazz, I watched, amazed, while Allison quickly learned the warmup routine without any hint of the challenges I'd had.

Next, she watched us practice our Duke Ellington piece. Although I stumbled through the last counts of the fast section, Allison never mentioned it. At the end of class, each group of girls performed their choreography and Miss Summers praised Faye on her hard-earned choreographic changes.

The four of us spent the rest of the day together. Our laughter filled the lounge and, with my friends surrounding me, I felt blissful, loved and accepted.

୬⊷ଢ଼

The following morning, after Mrs. Evans came for Allison, I gathered my costumes and dance bag for the trip to the gymnasium, where we met early, as planned, to rehearse Miss Summers's jazz piece. I still didn't know every step of the last thirty-two counts, but I pushed my fear away. Instead, I smiled and enjoyed myself while we practiced. *Could I do that during the performance?* I wondered.

The show was about to begin. I rushed off stage, changed into my ballet costume, double checked the elastic straps on my ballet shoes and returned backstage for the Mozart piece, which was third on the program. I heard the familiar sound of footsteps and muffled voices as people entered the gymnasium. I rubbed my sweaty palms against my skirt, hoping, without success, to calm down. I wondered if I would always feel this nervous before performing. The curtain opened and the beautiful waltz from *Sleeping Beauty* began. I caught glimpses of Daphne, the dancer who'd replaced Julia, performing the ballet solo as she twirled, on her toes, in and out of my vision. The audience erupted into loud applause when she ended with a set of difficult double pirouette turns. The second dance went by in a blur of movement and applause. Dancers rushed into the wings, brushing against me as I moved onto the stage in a dream-like state. The curtain opened and soft lavender light appeared. Suddenly, I was dancing, only aware of the music and my movements that flowed effortlessly and joyfully. During the grand jetés, at the music's crescendo, I flew into the air, suspended there for one long, glorious moment. Then, it was over. Beyond the stage lights I heard the audience clapping and shouting, "Bravo".

I fled to the locker room during the fourth dance. The jazz piece was next; *I had to hurry!* Faye and Cece pulled off my sweaty ballet costume and helped me tug on my jazz outfit. We left for the stage before my hat was securely pinned to my hair. Shaking, I thrust the last bobby pin in and prayed it would stay.

The Duke Ellington music started. We entered the stage. During the first section, I stayed right behind the lead dancer, feeling confident of the steps. Once the second section came, I blanked. What were the steps? My feet kept moving; I kept smiling; inside, I panicked. I managed to stay in my line, made my ending pose and curtsied on cue, exactly on time with the music.

Backstage, Miss Summers noticed my frown. Surprising me, she said, "Excellent job, Jo."

She couldn't mean it, I thought. Somehow I steadied my voice, "A good job of faking it, perhaps."

"You missed several steps. So what? It wasn't about the steps."

"What do you mean?"

"It was about you, your determination and your passion for dancing. The steps were only a small part of your camp experience. With more time, you'd have learned all eight counts in the fast section. I hope you'll return next summer."

I only said, "Not likely." I knew I would cry if I said more.

"That's a shame but you'll do well wherever you study. Best of luck," she said, wrapping me in her warm embrace. Deeply moved, I thanked her and left.

During intermission, I dressed for the "Bartered Bride Polka" with the level-3 dancers. I had no time to waste; our dance was first. I tugged at the bobby pins holding my hat in place, ripped it off and slid out of my jazz outfit. I was struggling to put on my tutu when Daphne approached. My sweaty hands fumbled while I attempted to attach a flower behind my ear. Noticing, Daphne took over, securing it for me. Looking into my eyes, she said, "Remember, you know the choreography well. So be confident out there."

I smiled broadly, thanked her and found my place on the stage. I heard the now familiar swish of the curtain and the music began. I'd grown to love the polka piece, rich with its rapid movements. Before I knew it, I was prancing about the stage in a stupor of joy. At the end of the middle section, I danced off the stage where I watched the ending from the wings. It was a flawless performance and the audience went wild! We returned to the stage for our bows. The applause continued so long it prompted Mr. Capp to join us on stage for our second bow. Energy coursing through my body, I felt like I was floating above the stage floor.

Back in the locker room, I disrobed, changed into my dress, collected my dance bag and costumes and hur-

ried to the gymnasium where I caught up with everyone. Dad took photographs of Cece, Faye, Allison, and
me posing together until Mrs. Evans stated that she
and Allison were headed home. I hugged them both
and thanked Mrs. Evans for making the long trip and
for bringing Allison.

A few minutes later, Mrs. Weir announced that the
buses were ready to take us back to camp where parents were to join us for a luncheon on the back lawn.

With the luncheon over, campers returned to their
rooms for their personal belongings. Then we would
meet Mrs. Weir in the lounge for the last time.

Upstairs, I sat on my bed, the room barren except for
my suitcases. Soon I would leave Briar Point Ballet
Camp and never return to this special time and place. A
sad, hollow feeling swept through me like an unwanted
wind. Yet, I reminded myself that my life had changed
and would keep changing. This summer, I'd become a
stronger dancer; my technique had greatly improved.
I'd confronted Julia and Mrs. Weir, made awesome
friends and met Stefan. A warm glow settled into that
hollow place as I glanced at my watch. Why was I daydreaming? Mrs. Weir expected us downstairs in five
minutes.

In the lounge, Mrs. Weir congratulated everyone at
Briar Point Ballet Camp on a wonderful show, handing
each of us a rose. I gave Mr. Capp and Miss Summers
hugs and thanked them for all they'd taught me.

Outside, girls and their parents carried suitcases and
trunks to their cars. Car doors slammed, engines start-

ed, and goodbyes were yelled. Faye, Cece, and I exchanged addresses, promised to write. We hugged an enormously long time as if trying to stop our inevitable departure. Then, pushing back tears, I headed to my parents' car. I turned around as we drove down the long winding hill, waving to Faye, Cece, and Briar Point Ballet Camp as they grew smaller and smaller before disappearing. Now, as I looked ahead, I wondered what new dance experiences awaited me.

Acknowledgments and Thanks

Very special thanks go to my late husband, Thomas Schwartz, for his encouragement, patience and hard work, which allowed me to teach dance and to write *Dancing, Suspended in Air*. I am forever grateful.

My sincere thanks go to my first editor and friend, Mr. John Horne, former editor at the *Boston Globe*, for his knowledge, guidance and belief in me. Thanks go to Bailey Regan, who was a fifteen-year-old ballet dancer and student with the Boston Ballet School when she read and commented on part one of *Dancing, Suspended in Air*. Her insight and knowledge greatly enhanced the story. I am extremely grateful to Mr. Horne and Ms. Regan. Their help was immeasurable.

So many people encouraged me along my writing journey that I can't name them all. However, some of them include the following: Tom Holbrook, editor at Piscataqua Press, for his excellent suggestions and guidance; Rebecca Gratwick, my sister, who read the picture book version and an earlier rendition of part one; Andre Dubus III, author and friend, for his constant encouragement and belief in my story from the beginning; Kristen Parker and Corinn Flaherty of the Salisbury, MA Public Library who helped me with computer issues; Maren Tirabassi, author and United

Church of Christ pastor, who read *Dancing, Suspended in Air*, made suggestions and encouraged me to publish; Susan Spellman, children's book illustrator, dancer and friend, who urged me to do my own illustrations; Bob Hoddeson and Jean Silverman, for their enthusiasm when my story was only one page; Carolyn Toloczko, dance teacher and friend, who posed for me and my aunt, Virginia Hatch, children's librarian.

GLOSSARY

*Please note that glossary words are underlined in the story.

1.) **Adagio** - A slow piece of music. Dancers' movements are slow and sustained during an adagio.

2.) **Allegro** - A fast piece of music. Dancers move quickly during an allegro.

3.) **Assemblé** - An assemblé is a jump in which the working foot slides along the floor and up into the air as the supporting foot pushes upwards. Both feet come together, landing on the floor at the same time. This step may be done in place or moving in different directions proceeded by a **glissade**.

4.) **Arabesque** - A position in which a dancer balances on the standing leg with the working leg extended up and behind.

5.) **Arms in first position** - To place the arms in a rounded position in front of, but not touching, the thighs.

6.) **Baby ballerina** - An extremely talented young ballet dancer, usually in her early teens, who performs with a company.

7) **Balancé** - A waltz step.

8.) **Ballet mistress** - A woman in a ballet company who gives classes and rehearses ballets in the company's **repertoire**, the ballets/dances that the company members know and perform.

9.) **Ballet mother** - A mother very involved in her daughter's or son's ballet career, usually watching classes on a regular basis.

10.) **Ballet practice record** - A record that contains music for practicing ballet exercises at the barre and center floor.

11.) **Barre** - A support, similar to a handrail, used to maintain balance as a dancer warms up, doing ballet exercises.

12.) **Bodice** - The top of a dress or costume, generally tight fitting.

13.) **Bravo** - An expression people in an audience yell to thank a dancer when he/she has given an exceptional performance.

14.) **Center floor** - Dance combinations done, away from the <u>barre</u>, in the middle of a dance studio.

15.) **Center stage** - The center part of a theatrical stage.

16.) **Changement** - A jump upwards from fifth position with the feet changing places in the air.

17.) **Choreography** - Choreography is the composition, or arrangement of steps, that forms a dance or dances. A choreographer is a person who creates dances and directs the movements of ballets or other forms of dance.

18.) **Combination/s** - The combining together of different steps in any dance form like jazz, ballet, modern, African etc.

19.) **Corps De Ballet** - The ballet dancers in a company who are not soloists.

20.) **Demi-plié** - To bend the knees in a turned-out position while the feet are kept flat on the floor.

21.) **Demi-point** - To rise up to the ball of the foot with the heel off the floor.

22.) **Développé** - A move in which the working leg moves up to the knee of the standing leg and slowly extends into the air where it is held. **Développé a la seconde**- is a **dévelopé** that is done to the side of the body.
23.) **Duet** - A dance for two dancers.

24.) **Fifth position (of the feet)** - A position of the feet in which the toes are turned out from the hips, away from the body. The heel of one foot is placed in front of the toes of the other and vice versa.

25.) **First position (of the feet)** - A position of the feet in which the legs are turned away from the center of the body. Each foot is turned toward ninety degrees as much as possible, with the heels of both feet touching.

26.) **Finale** - The last section of a dance or a ballet.

27.) **Fourth position (of the feet)** - A position of the feet similar to fifth position with a space between the front and back feet. The body's weight is evenly distributed over both feet.

28.) **Glissade** - A gliding step in which one foot generally slides to the side with the other foot sliding to it. This is a traveling step.

29.) **Grand plié** - A deep knee bend done with the legs in a turned-out position. In a grand plié, the knees bend so low that the heels lift off the floor verses a demi-plié in which the knees bend slightly and the heels stay on the floor. Often the word plié is used in coordination with another step, like a jump. In that case, a demi-plié is performed.

30.) Grand jeté - A large leap in which the legs separate into a forward split in the air.

31.) Grand battement - A large kick of the leg in which the knee is straight and the working foot slides off the floor in a pointed position. Grand Battement is done at the **barre** and at **center floor**, to the front, side or back.

32.) Jazz square - A step in which the feet form an imaginary square, either to the right or to the left.

33.) Jeté - A jump performed by brushing the working foot along the floor into the air causing a jump with a change of weight from one foot to the other.

34.) To **Mark** - To go through a dance without putting one's full energy into it. **Marking** is done before performing a ballet when a dancer uses his/her full energy. **Marking** is often done at a rehearsal to learn a new piece of choreography or to become acquainted with dancing on a new stage.

35.) Mambo - A jazz step in which the body remains in one place. With feet apart, and usually parallel, the body weight moves from one foot to the other by the bending of each knee, creating a swaying motion.
36.) On pointe - See Pointe Shoes for definition.

37.) Pas de bourrée - A traveling step in which the

feet change their position from fifth position with one foot front to fifth position with the other foot front.

38.) **Passé (sometimes seen without the accent mark)** - A position where the dancer balances on one leg while his or her working leg is bent upward and turned out at the hip. The foot touches the supporting leg to form a triangular shape.

39.) **Penché arabesque** - A movement, usually done by a woman, in which a dancer bends forward while maintaining an arabesque.

40.) **Piqué turn** - A traveling turn done on one leg. The ballet dancer steps up on the ball of the foot (in re-lévé) and spins while the other leg is held in the **passé** position. This can also be done in toe shoes, sometimes called pointe shoes, which allow the ballerina to balance on the tip of her toes verses the ball of the foot as in regular soft ballet shoes.

41.) **Pirouette** - A turn done in place with one leg held in passé as the dancer spins on the supporting leg using the ball of the foot. This turn is also done in toe shoes.

42.) **Pointe shoes** - Another name for toe shoes, pink satin shoes with a hard end that covers, protects and supports the toes. Toe shoes have a small flat bottom that allows the ballerina to balance on the tip of her toes. To be **on pointe (en pointe)** means to be up on toe shoes. A **pointe class** is a class taken while wearing toe shoes verses soft ballet slippers.

43.) To **Pose** - To maintain a position without moving.

44.) **Relevé** - To rise up onto the ball of the foot in soft ballet shoes or onto the tips of the toes when wearing toe shoes are worn. A **relevé arabesque** - a relevé done while in arabesque.

45.) **Révérence** - A curtsy at the end of a ballet class in appreciation of the teacher and/or an imaginary audience.

46.) **Sissonne ouverte a la seconde** - A jump from a fifth position **demi-plié** in which both feet move to the side but only one leg lands in a **demi-plié** while the other leg is held straight out in the air at the dancer's side.

47.) **Soloist** - A dancer who performs a **solo**, a dance for only one person.

48.) **Stage left** - The left side of the stage from the dancer's viewpoint, facing the audience. **Stage right** - The right side of the stage from the dancer's viewpoint.
49.) The **Standing** or the **Supporting leg/foot** - The leg/foot on which the dancer balances.

50.) **Step-ball-change** - A jazz step in which the body

weight goes onto one foot by bending the knee. Then the body weight shifts quickly to the ball of the other foot and back to the original foot.

51.) **Tendus** - Stretches done for both the leg and foot in which the foot extends as far as possible along the floor causing the foot to point.

52.) **Toe shoes** - Specially designed ballet slippers with reinforced toes for balancing on. Also see **pointe shoes** in this glossary for more detail.

53.) **Turned-out** - A position used to maintain balance with the legs turned out at the hips. Both legs and feet are turned away from the body's center as far as possible with each foot/leg aiming for a ninety degrees angle. A turned-out position can also be done sitting on the floor forming a side split.

54.) **Tutu** - A tutu is a short skirt worn by a ballerina that is made of netting that sticks out, often with a top layer of fabric such as satin.

55.) **Understudy** - A dancer who learns a piece of choreography so that he or she can dance it if the dancer for the part becomes injured or ill.

56.) The **Wings** of a stage - The curtains along the inside edges of the stage where dancers enter and exit.

Dancing, Suspended in Air

About the Author

Johanna Schwartz began ballet lessons at age six in Mrs. Cordova's Dancing School held in Durham, NH's Grange Hall. In August of 1963, she attended the Fokine Ballet Camp in Lenox, MA. At age fifteen, she taught for Mrs. Cordova and took classes at the Boston Ballet on Saturdays. The following summer, Johanna attended daily classes there. After high school, she apprenticed with the Boston Ballet, performed in several Nutcracker performances, took classes with members of the company and attended Boston University School of Fine Arts, earning a degree in Art Education. Johanna met her husband, Thomas, while in college and married him in 1974. They moved to Newburyport, MA where she taught ballet and creative dance classes to adults and children. Johanna also taught art to children in both public and private schools. Later in life, she became an occupational therapist assistant to children with special needs. Johanna now lives in Salisbury, MA with her two cats. She credits Mrs. Cordova with fostering her love of dance.

CPSIA information can be obtained
at www.ICGtesting.com
Printed in the USA
JSHW040016160920
7919JS00005B/14